Conflict at Chillicothe

Settlers of the Ohio Frontier

Karen Meyer

Sable Creek
PRESS

Cover and text design by Diane King, www.dkingdesigner.com
Flatboat photo © David Vaughn, www.tennesseedriftwood.com
Cover photo of Native American © Mark Stout - Fotolia
Back cover photo © Diane King, www.dkingdesigner.com

Scripture taken from the King James Version. Public domain.

Published by Sable Creek Press, PO Box 12217, Glendale, Arizona 85318
www.sablecreekpress.com

Meyer, Karen Ruth.
    Conflict at Chillicothe / Karen Meyer.
    p. cm.
    ISBN 9780976682325
[1. Frontier and pioneer life --United States --Fiction.. 2. Indians of North America --Fiction. 3. Frontier and pioneer life --Ohio --Fiction. 4. Christian fiction. 5. Historical fiction.] I. Title.

PZ7.M571712 Co 2010
[Fic]—dc22   2010930223

Printed in the United States of America.

Author's Note

Some of the characters you will meet in this story are fictional. Other characters' names appear in history books because they influenced the events of their times. This slice of our nation's early history gives a glimpse of the interaction between Ohio's Shawnee Indians and the white settlers who tamed the frontier.

Dedicated to the many brave settlers of the Ohio frontier.

May we be inspired by their example of trusting in God in life-challenging times.

Map of the Journey

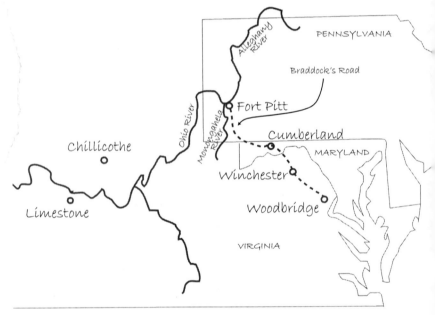

PENNSYLVANIA

Alleghany River

Braddock's Road

Ohio River

Monongahela River

Fort Pitt

Cumberland

Chillicothe

MARYLAND

Winchester

Woodbridge

Limestone

VIRGINIA

Contents

Author's Note 3

Glossary of Shawnee Words and Names 6

1 Uncle Philip's Visit.. 7

2 Looking Toward Limestone 17

3 Over the Mountains to Fort Pitt............................ 29

4 Flatboats on the Ohio 46

5 Uncle Philip's Stories.. 57

6 A Map of the Trip... 67

7 An Unexpected Journey 76

8 Two New Shawnee Braves..................................... 90

9 Attack of the Long-Knives 102

10 Homeward Bound... 111

11 Whithersoever Thou Goest................................ 124

Epilogue 129

Glossary of Shawnee Words and Names

Anequoi—squirrel meat

Chillicothe—The Place

Kumskaka—A-Cat-That-Flies-in-the-Air; one of a set of triplets; son of Pucksinwah and brother of Tecumseh

Lowaysica—also known as He-Makes-a-Loud-Noise; Shawnee prophet and medicine man; son of Pucksinwah; brother of Tecumseh; one of a set of triplets

Matchele ne tha-tha—you are my enemy

Msi-kah-mi-qui—the council house of the village

Nen-nemki—thunder

Ne-pah-loh—sleep

Oui-sah—good

Pasquawke—storm clouds

Peshewa—wildcat, bobcat

Pucksinwah—Shawnee chief; father of Tecumseh

Sauwaseekau—A-Door-Opened; warrior; one of a set of triplets; brother of Tecumseh

Shemanese—Americans; literally, Big Knives

Skillewaythetha—boy

Wasegeboah—Stand Firm; warrior

Wigewa—house

Wehpetheh—go, leave, depart

From *The Frontiersmen* by Allan Eckert
Printed 1967, by Little, Brown, and Company, Boston, Toronto
Used by permission

Chapter 1

Uncle Philip's Visit

"Why do I always have to take care of my little sister?" Joshua Stewart grumbled to himself. The two walked along a lane lined with Virginia's spring wildflowers. The tenant farmers' neat fields spread out on both sides of them as far as they could see. As they passed a trail leading to the wooded area beyond the fields, Joshua slowed down and his blue eyes brightened with an idea. *I'll just disappear into the woods, and Beka will have to find her own way home!*

"Joshua!"

He started, as if his nine-year-old sister could read his thoughts.

"Pa said you had to carry this empty bucket halfway home. Now it's your turn." The two had carried water to their father as he worked the soil for planting this year's crop of wheat.

"It's not halfway yet, Frizzle-top!" Joshua figured his sister might get mad enough to toss the bucket down and run ahead if he insulted her cloud of red-gold curls.

"It is, too! And *your* hair looks like … a straw pile … on a scarecrow!" Beka stamped her foot and tossed the bucket in her brother's direction. "You have to carry it now, or I'll tell Ma!" Then she turned and ran off toward home.

Joshua laughed to himself. *That worked well!* Then he shouted at his sister's back, "Go ahead, be a talebearer. But you might be a liar, too!"

Beka pretended not to hear him, and hurried down the lane. Before she'd gone very far, she turned and raced back toward her brother.

"What's the mat … " He stopped, alarmed, as he saw what his sister had seen. Far down the lane, two figures strode toward them. Joshua knew their stocky build and their jaunty walk—the Thrasher brothers!

Suddenly the warm spring day seemed chill, and Joshua had an urge to run. These two had reputations as trouble-makers among the farming families of their small community. Just last week they had tripped Joshua's friend Peter and kicked him until he was bleeding. Joshua ran toward his sister and grabbed her hand, pulling her toward the path leading to the woods.

"Quick, Beka! We can lose those two if we go home through the woods!"

"But … the bucket!"

"Oh, no! It's still where you threw it down! You run ahead, and I'll go back and get it."

Beka stood as if rooted, a look of fear on her face.

"Beka, you must run now! I'm faster than you; I'll catch up." As she turned to go, Joshua warned her, "Duck your head down as you run, so they can't see you."

With one backward glance at her brother, she took off down the twisting path. The tall weeds soon hid her from view. The

Thrasher brothers yelled some taunt at Joshua as he ran back and scooped up the bucket. They were still far enough away to ignore, but too close for him to follow Beka down the path.

I'll go back to the blackberry thicket we just passed. He raced there and crawled out of sight. Thorns ripped his hands and clothes, and his heart was racing. He waited, wondering if the bullies had followed Beka down the path.

Then he heard Isaac Thrasher complaining to his brother, "We missed our chance to whack him!"

"I told you we shoulda run after him, but you said it was too hot!"

Isaac continued to complain as the two walked on their way, but Joshua couldn't catch any more. He sucked in a deep breath, realizing he had stopped breathing.

I'd better wait a little longer, then cut through the fields to catch up with Beka. He grabbed the bucket and ran along the edge of the newly plowed earth. He was relieved to see his sister waiting under a pine tree.

"What happened?"

"Nothin'." Joshua didn't want to admit how scared he'd been. "Let's get on home."

"Your shirt's torn."

"So? Mind your own business."

They walked along in silence for a while. Beka flounced along the path, then stopped short. "Look! Spring beauties!" She bent down and picked a bouquet of the tiny pink wild-flowers.

Suddenly an insect flew across Joshua's path and landed in the weeds. It was an invitation he couldn't resist, even in his grouchy mood. He dropped the bucket and tried to catch the long-legged bug. It took him several tries, but finally he had his prize in hand.

"Joshua!" Beka called from further down the lane. "Leave those grasshoppers and come look. Somebody's coming to visit."

"Quit bein' so bossy. It's a katydid, anyway." Joshua grabbed the bucket and bounded after her. "Here, look." As soon as he opened his hand, the insect jumped right toward his sister.

"Aiee!" She squealed. "Joshua, quit. Now tell me who's riding toward our cabin."

She pointed to a large man on horseback with a bedroll behind his saddle.

"That's Uncle Philip!" He recognized the broad shoulders and red cheeks. "He was here a long time ago, remember? Ma's brother."

"Yes, I remember him, with his big moustache and his stories."

"He'll have some new stories, sure thing."

"Where's he been?"

"The frontier. All those tales he told about the Indians there made shivers go down my spine. Let's go!" The two raced toward their cabin.

They arrived just as their Grandma Sarah was opening the door to Philip's knock. She squealed like a schoolgirl when she saw her son. "Hallelujah! The Lord has brought you safely back to us."

Philip scooped her up and spun her around as if they were partners in a square dance. "Mama Sarah, you're a sight for sore eyes."

"Margaret, come see who's here." She brushed away a few tears from her eyes.

Margaret came in, wiping her hands on her apron. "Philip!" She practically shouted the name of her favorite brother. "It's been years."

"Four years," he laughed. "But you haven't changed a bit. You still look like my red-haired little sister." He turned to the children. "Joshua, you're a foot taller than when I was here last time." Joshua beamed and stood up a little straighter. "And, Rebekah." He pretended to be shocked. "Why, you were just a little bit of a thing, and now you're a young lady." Beka blushed and hid behind her mother. Philip looked around and then asked, "Margaret, where is that handsome rascal you married?"

"Still in the fields." Ma's shoulders sagged and she shook her head. "He works too hard. But when you're a tenant farmer with a family to feed …"

"That's just what I came here to change. I want you all to come to Limestone."

Joshua tugged at his mother's sleeve. "Ma, can I ring the bell for supper?" Ma nodded and waved him out the door.

"Now you sit down, Philip. Supper's almost ready. Mama Sarah and I were just mixing up the spoon bread. We'll talk about this Limestone idea when Mark comes."

Joshua returned and sat down beside his uncle. "Before Pa gets here, tell us where you've been since you were here last."

Uncle Philip laughed. "I don't suppose you two would like to hear a few stories?"

"Maybe not, if they're about Indians." Beka settled on the floor beside him.

"Tell us about the frontier!" Joshua said.

"The best of the frontier is Kentucky country. Still an untamed land. My cabin sets in the woods near a little settlement called Limestone." The two Stewart children leaned forward, not wanting to miss a single word. "One bone-cold night last winter, I heard my dogs barkin' fit to kill. I grabbed my rifle and went out to investigate. It was a pack of wolves! So hungry they came within a stone's throw of my cabin."

"Weren't you skeered?" Beka's eyes opened wide as she imagined the wolves.

"Naw, one rifle blast sent 'em high-tailin' it into the woods."

"Were they going to eat *you*, Uncle Philip?" Joshua asked.

"Naw, they were after my hogs! I lost one of the littlest ones the night before. Those wolves were just comin' back for a second helping of pork!" Philip roared at his own joke.

Just then, Pa strode in, hands dripping from washing the day's dirt off in the bucket outside. "Hey, Philip. What brings you to our doorstep?"

"Home cookin'. Mmm, just smell that Virginia ham. I can't wait to sink my teeth into it." Philip licked his lips in anticipation. "I've been cookin' for myself for so long I've forgotten what civilized food tastes like."

"So when are you goin' to get yourself a wife?"

Philip laughed. "Mark, you must be a mind reader." He gave his brother-in-law a playful push.

"Who's the lucky girl?" Pa asked.

"Her name is Susannah. I *hope* she is still back home. She may have gotten tired of waitin' for me to return from the wilderness."

"Uncle Philip, *I* would have waited for you," Beka said.

This brought a guffaw from him. "Why, thank you, Miss Rebekah."

"Last call for supper!" Ma set a pan of spoon bread down in the last open space left on the table. It was loaded with food the Stewart family had grown themselves.

"You don't need to call *me* twice, sister!" Philip tucked a napkin under his chin as he sat down at the plank table.

Pa bowed his head and asked the Lord to bless their food. Compliments flew as thick as flies on a horse for the fried ham and red eye gravy, greens, spoon bread, and dried-apple pie. Joshua laughed to himself. *Eatin' sure doesn't interfere with Uncle Philip's storytellin'! He just waves his knife and fork!*

Pa listened with special interest to his brawny brother-in-law. "How did you find this settlement—Limestone, it's called?"

"Men can claim land south of the Ohio River by just slashin' their mark into trees in the four corners of their property. So, two years ago I joined a party of settlers on a couple of flatboats, floatin' down the Ohio." Philip stretched out his arm as if to indicate the broad river. "Took us a week."

"Why were you having a party, Uncle Philip?" Beka wondered.

This brought a chuckle from Philip, but a "Hush, Rebekah," from her mother.

"Tell me honestly now," Pa said, "what about the danger from Indians?" At the mention of Indians, Joshua felt a prickle of fear down his spine. He glanced over at his sister. She'd grabbed Ma's dress and snuggled into it.

Philip leaned back. "The Kentucky lands are mostly safe for settlers since Colonel George Rogers Clark captured the

British posts of Kaskaskia and Vincennes. That was summer of '78, just last year."

"You mean the British are usin' the Indians to chase out the settlers?" Pa asked.

"The Indians are *supposed* to stay on the north side of the Ohio." He shook his head. "But yep, the guns and powder the Indians have are courtesy of King George."

Ma wondered, "Just where is your farm? Near the Ohio River?"

"Yes, Limestone sets where Limestone Creek pours into the Ohio. Right beside some steep cliffs—prettiest place for a settlement you ever saw. My claim's 'bout three miles from the landin'."

"Have you grown any crops yet?" Pa asked.

"Only five of my hundred acres 're cleared, but last fall I got forty bushels an acre on the three I had in corn."

"Forty bushels an acre!" Pa whistled in admiration.

"Is there any more land left to claim in the Limestone area?" Ma asked.

"Do pigs have curly tails? Beyond our settlement you can walk for miles and never see another cabin."

Joshua had listened with increasing excitement as his uncle spoke. "Are we goin' to Limestone, Pa?"

"I've always said someday I'd quit this place. But I'm a farmer, not a frontiersman," Pa said.

"Nonsense," Philip said. "You've got more experience than half the settlers I've seen." He pounded the table, making Beka jump. "Besides, we all help each other. *And* we've got Simon Kenton."

"Who's he?"

"He's the best woodsman in the Kentucky territory. Knows the land like the back of his hand. I want you to meet him. Trouble is, he went off huntin' a few months before I left and hasn't been seen since."

"So Kenton, the best woodsman in the territory, has got himself lost?" Pa chuckled.

Philip hesitated and rubbed his chin. "There've been rumors the Shawnees captured him."

Ma gulped. "Are the Indians coming all the way to Limestone?"

Joshua added, "I don't want to meet up with any Indians, Pa."

Philip tried to explain. "The settlement needed some food, so he and two others went where the game was, across the Ohio into Indian territory."

Ma said, "If there are Indians, it's too dangerous for Mama Sarah."

"Fiddlesticks! If you go, I'm going along!" Grandma sputtered.

"It would be a really hard life …" Pa began.

"So is growing wheat," Ma pointed out.

Pa took Ma's hand. "What do you think we ought to do, Margaret?"

Ma was silent for a while, thinking of the dream they'd had of going to the frontier, their promised land. They named their firstborn son Joshua for that reason. Finally she said, "We want our own farm, our own house. It may be dangerous, but the Lord can take care of us. I think He is giving us a nudge."

Pa nodded in agreement. "I've worked for a landlord for fourteen years and I'm ready to head west."

"I plan to return to Limestone with my bride next spring. We could meet at Fort Pitt and buy a flatboat together," Philip said.

"When?"

"Early May. The mountain roads oughta be passable by then."

"We'll pray about it and send word about our decision." Pa's eyes were sparkling. "Margaret is right. I believe the Lord has given us a road sign pointin' west."

Joshua shivered, even though the cabin was warm. He couldn't tell if it was from excitement or fear. *Maybe we're headin' to the Kentucky frontier!*

Chapter 2

Looking
Toward Limestone

"Grandma," Joshua looked up from the stick he was whittling, "what will it be like livin' in Limestone?" Joshua had thought of little else during the months since Uncle Philip's departure.

Joshua could tell Grandma was thinking, because her rocker stopped squeaking, then she began again. "From what Philip said, there are thirty, forty other families in the settlement …"

"So there would be children for Beka and me to play with." Joshua whittled the stick to a sharp point. "But could we play outside without gettin' scalped or something?"

The question hung between them as Grandma continued knitting and rocking. "Let's not borrow trouble. The good Lord knows what He has planned for us, Joshua. I'm sure I don't."

Joshua bit his lower lip. "Sometimes I think I don't want to go to Limestone."

Grandma nodded and smiled. "Going somewhere new is a bit scary …"

"Yeh, 'specially if there's Indians."

"But if you know you're following the Lord …"

Joshua looked doubtful. "Pa said the Lord had given him a road sign pointin' west." He continued shaving the stick until it was nearly gone. "But the Lord hasn't told me anything."

"Yes, He has. Look in Ephesians … it says, 'children, obey your parents.'"

Joshua frowned.

"Let me tell you about your grandpa." Grandma put down her knitting and leaned back with a faraway look in her eyes. "My Richard was the first one in his family to leave the old country." The rocker squeaked rhythmically as she retold the family history. "Sixteen years old he was when he said goodbye to his mother and father. He had two sisters and three brothers, all younger." Grandma smiled as Joshua's eyes brightened.

"Grandpa was sure brave." Joshua had heard these stories for all of his twelve years, yet he always had new questions. "He lived in England, right? Tell me about his long boat ride across the ocean," he begged.

"His mother made him a cloth bag and packed it full of bread and cheese. He still ran out of food two days before they landed. But God sent him a fish. A seabird dropped it right on his head!"

"Just like God fed Elijah."

Grandma nodded. "When he got to Virginia, Richard had to work a year for the man who bought his ticket. Then he headed west and walked until he came to our house." Grandma smiled as she came to this part of the story. "I saw him walking up the road and I just *knew* God was sending me a husband."

"Did he ask you to marry him right away?" Joshua asked.

"Oh, child! He had no money to care for a wife and family. He worked for a year and a half for my father before he was brave enough to ask him to let us be married." Grandma picked up her Bible and turned the pages as if they were old friends. "Genesis twelve, verse one says, 'Get thee out of thy country, and from thy kindred, and from thy father's house, unto a land that I will show thee.' That verse sent your grandpa on his journey. He felt the *Lord* was telling him to leave England."

Joshua had never known his grandpa, yet he felt he knew all about him because of all Grandma's stories.

"Now, your Pa has been talking about going west ever since you were born. He has had one thing after another to keep him from going, but now the Lord wants him to go. So the Lord will show the way for the whole family."

"And will He help me be as brave as Grandpa?" Joshua asked.

"Of course." As she had often done before, Grandma placed her gnarled hand on Joshua's shoulder. "Let's pray about it right now. Lord, you have big plans for Joshua and our family. Use him for your service, Lord. Keep him safe; help him to be a brave leader. Show him …"

"Mama Sarah, Joshua! Come quick!" Ma's shouts came from outside. Joshua ran out and Grandma hobbled behind as fast as she could go.

"What's wrong? What happened?" he shouted.

Ma stood at the well. The heavy wooden cover and stone had been pushed to one side. The bucket lay on its side, and water was splashed all around. " Rebekah fell down the well! She was helping me get a bucket of water …"

"Maaamaa … help!" A cry came from the opening of the well.

"Beka!" Fear gripped Joshua as he ran to the opening. *It's so far to the bottom. Beka looks so little. What if she's hurt?* Pa had always said, "It's your job to protect your sister." A feeling of helplessness washed over him. His knees wobbled.

"How can we get her out?" Grandma joined Joshua and Ma at the edge of the well.

Ma shook her head. "I d-don't know!"

"I … I could go down to get her, Ma."

"Let's tie the rope around him," Grandma said, "then lower him down by the crank."

As soon as Ma tied the rough rope around his middle, Joshua's knees began to shake. "What happens when I get to the bottom?"

"I don't know. The Lord will help you figure it out," Ma said.

"We'll be praying, too," Grandma said.

Joshua took a deep breath and grabbed the rope. He braced his feet against the side and slowly inched toward his sister.

"Are you hurt, Beka?" Joshua asked as he neared her.

"Owwwoww. My arm hurts," she wailed. She clung to a narrow ledge, and the water was up to her waist. A cut over one eye was bleeding.

What should I do next? I know. Beka can ride up in the bucket. Joshua joined her on the ledge and untied himself. "Ma, pull up the rope and send it back down with the bucket!"

"It's goin' to be all right, Beka." Joshua put his arm around his sister's shoulder.

Tears rolled down Beka's cheeks. "I'll never get out of here!"

"Look! Ma's sendin' down the bucket."

"You mean …?"

"Yes, you get to ride in it."

Beka's eyes widened.

"You'll have to squat down with the handle between your legs." Joshua held the bucket on the ledge and helped his sister climb in. "Now, Beka, pretend this is a fun ride, and we're playin' a game."

Through her tears, Beka managed the littlest bit of a smile. "Can I close my eyes?"

"That's a good idea. Just remember to hold on tight to the rope with both hands. Pull up the bucket now, Ma."

The crank creaked as Beka rose slowly toward the light. When the rope came back down without the bucket, Joshua carefully tied it around his middle again. He called for the crankers to do their job a second time. Grandma and Ma grunted together. The crank complained more loudly than before, but Joshua made it to the top.

Everyone laughed, cried, and talked at once, except Beka. She looked bewildered. Ma put an arm around her. "Let's get you into the cabin for some clean, dry clothes. We'll have to see if that arm needs a splint, too."

"I'll put some of my marigold salve on that cut above your eye, Rebekah," Grandma declared. "That'll put it all to rights."

When Pa came home, each one told him part of the story of Rebekah's rescue from the well. Pa clapped Joshua on the back. "Son, I'm proud of you. When I'm off in the fields, it's great to have a man in the house."

"I was too upset to think clearly," Ma said. "If Joshua hadn't thought of the bucket …" Her voice trailed off and she shook her head.

"I might still be down there," Beka finished for her.

Joshua was pleased but a bit embarrassed by all the praise. Grandma leaned over and spoke just so he could hear. "The Lord is already answering my prayer. You were a brave leader today, Joshua."

In the fall, the whole family helped cut the wheat and bind it into sheaves. After the grain had dried, it was threshed and poured into cloth sacks. As Pa headed to nearby Dumfries to sell the grain, he said, "If there's enough money left over after paying rent on the farm, we'll leave in the spring for the frontier."

When Pa returned from the trip, he couldn't wait to share the good news. "Margaret! Joshua and Rebekah! Mama Sarah!" he hollered for them before he was even out of the wagon.

"Mark, your smile is as bright as a Virginia sunrise," Ma said.

Pa waved the money in the air. "We can go to Limestone!"

Beka jumped up and down with excitement.

"The Lord has provided what we need, as He always does," Grandma said.

Joshua smiled, but inside he had a fluttery feeling. *What about those Indians Uncle Philip talked about?*

"I'll have to give the landlord notice," Pa said.

"And we'll have to send word to Philip," Ma added.

"We have six months to get ready and lots to do," Pa said. "We'll have to decide what to take, and sell the rest."

"And buy supplies for the frontier," Ma said.

"We can buy supplies in Fort Pitt, and we won't have to drag 'em up and down all those mountains in Pennsylvania."

"Oh, Mark. This is such a big decision," Ma said. "I'm worried."

"Whoa!" Pa held up his hand. "Remember, we prayed the Lord would give us the money, and if He did, we'd *know* ..."

"That God wants us to go west," Ma finished for him. "I know, but ..."

Joshua spoke up. "I know how Ma feels. Thinkin' about the dangers scares me too, even though we *know* God wants us to go to Limestone."

Grandma settled it. "Danger is just the Lord's way of giving us a chance to trust Him."

The six months' preparation time whizzed by. One bright May morning, Ma called up to Joshua and Rebekah in the loft. "Roll out of bed, you sleepy-heads! We leave today, and there's plenty to be done."

Joshua sat up so quickly he almost hit the slanted ceiling. Beka asked, "What's the matter?"

"I've just had an awful dream. We were bein' chased by Indians!"

"We, the whole family?"

"No, just you and me."

"Did we get away?"

"I don't know. You were cryin' because I'd tripped and fallen down. The Indians were gettin' closer, and closer ... and then I heard Ma callin' us to get up."

Ma called again. "Bring all your bed clothes down with you when you come."

Beka hopped out onto the rough wooden floor and folded her quilt. Joshua continued to stare off into the distance. "I could see their painted faces."

"We'll see *real* Indians when we get to Limestone, won't we?"

Joshua finally climbed out of bed and began rolling up his blankets. "We'll see Indians lots sooner than that. Uncle Philip said there are Indians at Fort Pitt."

"Joshua." Ma was calling again. "Bring those mattress ticks down and empty the straw out back. When you're done, come get your ham and grits."

"Yes, Ma," he called back, making a face at Beka. They both laughed and scurried to complete their chores, as they pushed aside all thoughts of Indians.

By the time the two had finished chores and breakfast, a knot of neighbors had gathered to wish them well on their journey. Peter's ma brought a checked cloth wrapped around a batch of johnnycake. Peter motioned to Joshua to hold out his hand and pressed a small white object into it. The flattened oval showed a three-masted sailing ship on a stormy sea.

"Oooh!" breathed Joshua. "It's …"

"Scrimshaw, scratched on whalebone," Peter finished for him. "My uncle's first mate on a ship just like that."

A lump rose in Joshua's throat. "Thanks! I … I won't forget you!" After an awkward pause, Peter turned to go.

"Wait! I have something my Uncle Philip gave me. I want you to have it … to remember me by." Joshua quickly untied a soft deerskin bag from his belt. "It's got a few green rocks in it now, but you can put whatever you want in it."

Joshua took one last look around. He wanted to remember everything. Their cabin with the well out back where he had rescued Beka, the orchard beyond where he and Peter had climbed the biggest tree and talked of what they'd do when they were older; Ma's garden where she grew lots of food for their family. *It's the last time I'll see all this.*

"Joshua." Beka's voice broke into his musings. "Are you gonna grow roots there or come with us?" She was already in the wagon, and Pa was motioning to him to get in, too.

He quickly climbed in and squeezed in beside her. "It's sure crowded in here." Joshua looked at the change in their old farm wagon, as if noticing it for the first time. Pa and Ma had transformed it into a home on wheels. Pa had arched hickory branches over the top and Ma had sewed white canvas for a roof. All of their furniture was gone, sold … except for Grandma's rocking chair. There it was, strapped to the back, right next to the chickens. Their cow was tied to the back right behind the box Pa had built to carry all the tools. The food, kitchen stuff, bedding and clothes, and all sorts of supplies were stashed in every corner. Joshua felt it pushing into him on all sides. *And, there's a heavy weight on my chest.*

Pa was praying for God to watch over them on their journey. The tightness in Joshua's chest eased. He smiled and waved to the crowd. He held up his scrimshaw toward Peter, and Peter waved the deerskin bag. Joshua turned and looked ahead. Maybe this trip wouldn't be so bad after all. *It will probably hold lots of excitement and surprises, just like one of Uncle Philip's stories.*

Joshua and Beka had never traveled far from home. They enjoyed seeing the beautiful Virginia countryside. The road passed through little villages with neat houses. Mothers were already hanging wash on their clotheslines; Ma called out a cheerful greeting to them and they waved back.

All along the way, men plowed their fields with teams of horses. Pa always waved, and the men waved back. Children played outside. They waved back at Joshua and Beka. In the distance to their right, they caught glimpses of the wide Potomac River sparkling in the early morning sunshine.

"There's the road to Dumfries," Pa pointed. "This fall I won't be takin' my grain to market there." He turned and smiled at Ma. "We'll find out how well Virginia wheat grows in Kentucky."

After their brief stop for a cold lunch, Beka said, "Let's play a game."

Joshua thought for a while. "How about playin', I'm goin' to London, but say, 'I'm goin' to Limestone.'"

"Limestone. Good. And whatever we take along has to be something we're really taking."

Joshua laughed. "You always like to make up new rules. All right, I'll start with the letter A. I'm goin' to Limestone, and I'm takin' an axe."

"I'm going to Limestone, and I'm taking an axe and a Bible."

Grandma Sarah turned and said, "That's everything you'll need to tame the wilderness. Can I play?" Beka and Joshua nodded. "I'm going to Limestone and I'm taking an axe, a Bible, and some candles, so I can read my Bible, of course."

Pa said, "I want to go on this trip, too! I'm goin' to Limestone and I'm takin' an axe, a Bible, some candles, and a dog."

"Pa," Beka said, "Only say what we're really taking."

"Since we'll be in the wilderness, we'll need a dog, so I was plannin' to buy one, maybe at Fort Pitt."

"Really?" Joshua grinned. "I've always wanted a dog. What kind will it be?"

"The Lord knows," Pa replied. "But I don't."

"We'll just pray He'll provide us a good dog," Grandma added.

"Now it's my turn, right?" Ma said. "I'm going to Limestone and I'm taking eggs."

"You forgot all the other stuff to take, Ma," Joshua pointed out.

"Oh, that's right. Let's see … I'm going to Limestone and I'm taking an axe, a Bible, … some candles, a dog, and some eggs. I figure since we got chickens, then we'll have eggs."

"Finally, my turn again," Joshua smiled. "I'm goin' to Limestone and I'm takin' an axe, a Bible, some candles, a dog, some eggs, and … a fryin' pan—to cook the eggs in."

"I'm going to Limestone and I'm taking an axe, a Bible, some candles, a dog, some eggs, and a frying pan, and … Grandma!" Rebekah gave Grandma Sarah a big grin.

"You'd better not leave me home!" she hugged her grand-daughter.

Pa began, "I'm goin' to Limestone and I'm takin' all that stuff …"

"Pa! You hafta say it all, or you're out," Beka said.

"All right, little miss. I'm goin' to Limestone and I'm takin' an axe, a Bible, some candles, a dog, some eggs, a fryin' pan, Grandma, and a hoe."

"Good, because I want to have a garden," Ma said. "So, I'm going to Limestone, and I'm taking an axe, a Bible, some candles, a dog, some eggs, a frying pan, Grandma, a hoe, and ink."

"I'm glad you didn't say Indians, Ma, 'cause I couldn't think of anythin' else." Joshua said. "I'm goin' to Limestone and I'm takin' an axe, a Bible, some candles, a dog, some eggs, a fryin' pan, Grandma, a hoe, some ink, and, let's see … johnnycake. Just like Peter's ma gave us for our lunch today."

The travelers continued around, with everyone successfully adding to the list. Finally, it was Joshua's turn for the last letter of the alphabet. "Z is too hard!" he exclaimed. He thought for several minutes as the horses plodded along. Finally, he fairly shouted, "Zeke!"

"Who's Zeke?" Beka demanded.

"Guess!" was the mysterious reply.

"Someone's name?"

"Yes."

"He has to be coming with us."

"Yes."

"But not with us now?"

"No, not yet."

"At Fort Pitt?"

"Yep, Pa said so."

At this, Beka brightened. "I know, the dog!"

"Right. We'll name him Zeke," Joshua laughed.

"What if we get a female dog?" Pa asked.

Beka had the solution. "We'll just call her Zekah, then."

Chapter 3

Over the Mountains to Fort Pitt

"Mark, how far is it to Fort Pitt?"

"Now, Margaret, we just got a good start on this trip."

"I'm not fretting. I just want to know."

"Me too, Pa," Joshua said.

Pa rubbed his chin and pursed his lips, thinking. "I asked Philip last year, and he guessed it was about two hundred and fifty miles."

"Oh, *that* far!" Ma groaned.

"Said it took him only six days, though." Pa laughed, "But that was on horseback."

"So how much longer will it take in a wagon?"

"The Lord knows. We may have to wait for a flooded river to go down. We may have to sit tight while a storm blows over. We may have to …"

"Mark, you could guess," Ma pleaded.

Pa continued as if he hadn't even heard. "And it's spring-time. Roads in Pennsylvania 're no doubt muddy, probably have trees across 'em from the winter storms … the Lord knows what we'll meet up with."

"Mercy me. I give up!" Ma raised both hands in the air. "I guess we'll get there when we get there."

"That's true," Grandma said. "And even truer, we'll get there when the Lord wants us to get there. But, Mark, tell us how many miles we might make on a good day."

Pa tilted his hat back so he could think better. "Today's been a good day so far, and if we keep movin' till suppertime … mebbe we'll make thirty miles."

The Stewart family made good time on the roads through Virginia. However, the flatter lands near the Potomac River gradually gave way to hillier country as they headed inland. The first real mountain came just before the city of Winchester. The horses strained to pull the heavy wagon up the long slope.

"Time to get out and walk, 'cept you, Grandma Sarah," Pa said.

"I can walk with the rest of you," Grandma said. "While the Lord gives me two legs that work, I plan to use 'em."

Joshua and Beka were glad to stretch their legs. They scampered ahead of the wagon, eager to see what might be ahead. When they reached the top of the slope, both of them stopped to stare. Far below, smoke rose from rows and rows of cabins.

"What a pretty sight," Beka said. "Do you suppose that's Winchester?"

"It has to be."

They raced back, each wanting to be first to tell the news.

"Pa, Winchester's just over the top of the mountain!" Joshua shouted.

"There's too many cabins to even count," Beka added, out of breath.

"Maybe we'll make it beyond Winchester a ways, then," Pa replied. "It's the skinny side of noon."

When the wagon reached the summit, Pa stopped and got out his axe. "C'mon, Joshua, we'll cut down one of those good-sized trees."

"What for, Pa?"

"Take a look at that steep slope to Winchester. We'll tie the tree to our back axle to keep the wagon from goin' faster than the horses," Pa said.

When the tree was in place, Pa set both brakes and they all climbed into the wagon. Ma worried they were going to slide over the cliff beside the road. Beka grabbed her brother's arm and sucked in her breath. Pa just smiled and started singing a silly song with the refrain, "Up the mountain they did go, down again, with a Hey! Ho!" He kept making up new verses until they were all laughing.

Storefronts lined both sides of the main street of Winchester, with displays of everything from dry goods to hardware to staple food items. People nodded to the Stewarts from the board sidewalks. Horses waited patiently, tied to a railing or a nearby tree. The family stopped to eat the breakfast leftovers and fill their jugs at the public pump. Nearby a knot of men stood talking in front of a blacksmith shop. Pa and Joshua walked over to ask a few questions.

"How's the road to Pennsylvania?" Pa asked.

One big-bellied man laughed loudly, showing a missing front tooth. "It's a long way to Pennsy! Better get yourselves to Cumberland, Mary-land, first."

"That's fine with us," Pa said. "Any mountains between here and Cumberland?"

"Yup. A good-size one, too." The man laughed again. "But the road takes the long way 'round it."

"That's fine with us, too," Pa said. "How far is it?"

Another man spoke up. "It's about sixty miles. The road's not too bad, 'specially compared to what you'll find t'other side of Cumberland."

Pa winced a bit at this news. "Oh? What should we expect?"

"Get your axes sharpened," the big-bellied man said, and laughed loudly again. He sounded very unfriendly to Joshua, but Pa didn't seem to mind.

The other man said, "Old Gen'l Braddock and his army were in a hurry to get to Fort Doo-Caine. It's Fort Pitt now. Anyway, they chopped that road right through some purty thick woods and some of them trees are a-growin' again."

Pa smiled at both men. "Thanks for the tip." He lifted his hat and nodded.

"Good thing Ma wasn't with us, right Pa?" Joshua asked as they walked back to the wagon.

Pa nodded and smiled a knowing smile.

"Look ahead, younguns," Pa called out one morning. They had left Winchester behind them as the road continued to climb. Far ahead, a heavily wooded mountain seemed to block their way. "The first of the Appalachians."

"How will we ever get over it?" Ma asked.

"The road will curve around and find the best way for us—all we need to do is follow."

"Sounds like Bible advice," Grandma said.

"Pa, how many mountains do we have to cross before we get to Fort Pitt?" Joshua asked.

"Son, I'm not exactly sure; maybe six or eight. How 'bout if you keep count?"

"Me, too! Can I help?" Beka asked.

Joshua almost snapped a quick "no," but caught himself. Pa had given him a stern talking-to back when the Thrasher brothers had nearly caught them on the road. His resentment of being his little sister's caretaker had nearly gotten them both into trouble. Pa had showed him the Bible story of Cain and Abel. Cain had asked God, "Am I my brother's keeper?" Pa's question, "You don't want to be anythin' like the first murderer, do you?" had stuck with him ever since.

Trying to be glad that he was Beka's "keeper," Joshua answered his sister, "Sure, Beka, you be the one that marks them down."

The advice the men in Winchester had given was right. The road to Cumberland had been kept up well and the travelers had no problems. As they sat by the fire that night, Pa took out his axe and Joshua's hatchet, and sharpened them. He winked at Joshua as he explained to Ma he just wanted to be ready in case there were any trees blocking the way.

Joshua smiled in anticipation. He liked chopping down trees—it made him feel like a real frontiersman. He remembered Uncle Philip talking about clearing land to plant corn.

Ma added wood to the fire and sat down by Rebekah, who snuggled up close to her.

"Will we be able to plant a little garden as soon as we get to Limestone?" Ma asked.

"Maybe so, Margaret. Building us a cabin will come first, but …"

"I can help, Pa," Joshua said.

"Listen." Beka held up her hand. Everyone strained to hear anything unusual besides the crackling of the fire and the spring peepers in the nearby pond.

"I hear a screech owl, way off," Grandma offered.

"No, it's a whimpering." Beka tilted her head to try to catch the sound again. No one said anything as they listened.

"Yes, I hear it too," Joshua said.

"Get your gun, Mark," Ma said. "It's probably some wild animal."

"Lord, protect us," Grandma said. "Let's get into the wagon."

"I want to know what it is," Joshua said.

"Maybe I'll wait until mornin' and then scout around …"

"Mark, now would be better," Ma said. "Children, get into your beds; it's time you were asleep anyway."

"Aww, I'm not sleepy," Joshua said.

"I'm too scared to go to sleep," Beka added.

"Hush, children. Just obey." Ma helped them into the wagon. Pa got his gun out from its place behind the seat and loaded it. Grandma added more wood to the fire and then joined them in the wagon. They watched Pa walking slowly in the direction of the noise. He quickly disappeared from the circle of firelight.

They waited and listened. There it was, the whimpering noise again. Then they heard Pa's voice. "What do we have here?"

Pa came back to the fire carrying something in his arms. Joshua leaned out, trying to figure out what it was.

"Come out here, everyone," Pa said. "Come see the wild animal."

"It's a puppy," Joshua said.

"What's wrong with its paw?" Beka saw the half-grown pup's right front paw swollen to twice the normal size. The poor animal whined in pain. Beka reached out to pat the puppy.

"Don't touch it, Rebekah," Ma warned. "It may bite."

"I think it may have tangled with a porcupine," Pa said. "See that broken-off quill in the toe-pad? I'll have to cut it out. It has a barb on the end, like a fishhook."

Grandma looked at the sad creature's paw. "Poor puppy; it's probably infected. When you're done, I'll put a poultice of garlic and bread on it to draw out the poison."

"Can I make a bed for him, Ma?" Beka asked.

Ma rolled her eyes and sighed. "I suppose. Let's get some of the rags we packed."

The puppy, Zeke, of course, whimpered as Pa cut out the quill. Grandma doctored and bandaged the paw and Joshua gave Zeke some of the leftover stew from supper. Zeke settled onto his bed, wagged his curly brown tail, sighed, and soon was sound asleep.

"*Now* are you sleepy, you two?" Ma asked. "Off to bed."

"Ma, do you suppose God sent us that puppy?" Joshua asked.

Pa answered before Ma could say a word. "Of course God sent Zeke to us. Grandma prayed for a dog. It's amazin' how fast God answered that prayer."

The next night as Ma and Rebekah gathered up the plates to wash, Zeke pricked up his ears. He barked as he peered down the road. Horses emerged from the twilight carrying two bearded men wearing wide brimmed hats. Both men carried guns and had knapsacks and blankets behind their saddles.

Pa walked out to meet them. "Ho there, strangers! Where're you headed?"

The men came closer; the taller one answered, "Fort Pitt. Mind if we warm ourselves by your fire a spell?"

"The two of you are most welcome," Pa replied, nodding. "We have a bit of supper left to share if you're hungry."

They both dismounted and staked their horses to graze. Ma quickly filled two plates with stew from the kettle near the fire.

The two ate hungrily. Joshua noticed they didn't even bow their heads to pray before wolfing down the food. *They talk with their mouths full, too. Ma never lets me do that.* As he listened to them talk, Joshua felt very uncomfortable, though he couldn't say why. The taller one spoke for both of them. "We're headed west. There a man can earn his fortune without worryin' about the law. There's free land in the Ohio River Valley and the huntin' and trappin' is easy."

Ma came over and rounded up the youngsters. "Off to bed, you two."

Joshua knew better than to argue, but the talk was just getting interesting. Joshua lifted the edge of the canvas beside his bed, and he could still hear what they were saying. Pa and the men sat around the fire for an hour trading stories.

The men described an Indian raid on a new settlement, telling many gruesome details. Joshua clutched his stomach and dropped the flap, wishing he hadn't listened. Finally, the men left the fire and rolled up in their blankets.

Joshua lay awake. The vivid description of a settler being scalped would not leave his mind. Far off in the woods, a whippoorwill called ... whip, whip, whip-poor-will.

Lord, please protect us when we get to Limestone. Finally, the ugly pictures in his mind faded and he fell asleep.

The two men rode off early the next morning without so much as a wave. Joshua was glad to see them go. Not long after, the Stewart wagon lumbered onto the road. The road, however, nearly disappeared a few miles beyond where they had camped. Pa guessed it hadn't been used by a wagon for eight or ten months. Pa unhitched the horses and put them to graze. Then he got out the axe and hatchet. Soon the second-growth saplings were falling left and right, with just a few swings of Pa's axe.

"Pa, my hatchet just doesn't work as well as your axe," Joshua said.

Pa chuckled. "You're doin' just fine, son. Keep on choppin'! If we want to make Fort Pitt to meet Uncle Philip, we'll have to make better time than we have so far today."

The two continued to hack a trail for their wagon. The sun rose higher in the sky and Joshua's arms began to ache. *Pa always says to whistle when I feel like complainin', but my mouth's too dry to whistle.*

Way back down the road, the wagon was still barely visible. Joshua watched Beka and Zeke playing under a nearby tree. Then he saw a movement beyond their wagon, something white. "Pa! There's another wagon comin' along the road!"

Pa pushed his hat back a bit and wiped his brow. "It's time we took a rest anyway. Let's head back."

The horses nickered a greeting to the sturdy team coming toward them. The driver, a stocky man wearing a wide-brimmed black hat, waved to the Stewarts. Beside the man sat his plump wife holding a baby in her arms. The woman wore a long plain dress, and covered her hair neatly with a white bonnet. A large black dog walked by the back wheel of the wagon.

Zeke began to bark excitedly as Pa waved to them and called, "Ho, there!"

The man smiled, nodded, and introduced himself and his wife as Elijah and Rachel Hartman. After Pa explained the situation, Mr. Hartman got out his axe and joined Pa and Joshua. The three went to work cutting the road without talking very much. Joshua led the way, clearing the saplings with a few well-placed chops. Pa and Mr. Hartman worked on opposite sides of the road. They had a friendly competition going on, each one trying to stay ahead of the other. When the sun began to slip behind the hills in the west, Pa declared it was time to quit for the day.

Joshua's arms ached and both hands had blisters, but he smiled to himself in spite of it. Pa called him their trailblazer and said he'd set the pace for the three of them.

After dinner, everyone sat around the fire talking. Mr. Hartman and Pa talked about their farms. Mr. Hartman had inherited half a small farm the previous year when his father died. "W-when my b-brother offered to b-buy me out, I didn't d-deliberate long! Th-that land was r-rocky and w-worn out! S-so Rachel and I s-sold our possessions and s-said our good-byes …"

"It was hard leaving all our kin," Rachel said. "We may never get back east; baby Jacob will probably never know his grandparents." She rocked him gently and smiled down at his chubby face.

Grandma Sarah reached out to hug Joshua and Rebekah. "The Lord has blessed me by letting me come along on this trip."

The fire burned low. Ma stood and directed her two youngsters to bed. Rebekah jumped up and headed toward the wagon.

"Ma, can't I stay up a little longer?" Joshua asked. "Please?"

Pa nodded to Ma. "We men have some things to discuss."

Joshua stood taller, wondering what Pa needed to talk about.

After the women had gone, Pa asked, "Elijah, what have you heard about the Indians on the frontier?"

Mr. Hartman kept his voice low as he added a few pieces of wood to the fire. "Th-the land n-north of the Ohio R-river has p-plenty of Indians! F-five d-different tribes, I h-hear. The Sh-Shawnees are the l-largest and most f-fearsome."

"But my brother-in-law told me the Kentucky lands were fairly safe for settlement, south of the Ohio."

"Th-that's true. B-but Indians s-sometimes send r-raiding parties across the r-river."

"Raiding parties. Are they mostly after horses?"

"H-horses are one thing. S-sometimes they might be r-retaliation for s-somethin' the w-whites have d-done to them r-recently."

Pa shook his head sadly. "Nobody wins, then." He reached down to pat Zeke, who sat with his head on Joshua's lap. "Where do you plan to settle your family?"

"W-we're not exactly s-sure."

"If you decide to settle in Limestone, we'd be pleased to have you as neighbors."

"Th-Thanks. R-Rachel and I were w-waiting till we got to F-Fort Pitt to decide where to s-settle."

Way off in the distance, Joshua saw a jagged streak brighten the sky. "Pa, look at the lightnin."

Distant thunder rumbled as Pa stood up. "We'd better tie down the flaps tonight."

Joshua liked the sound of the rain hitting the canvas top of their wagon. Gusts of wind whistled through the space near his head, sprinkling his face with cool raindrops. As he dropped off to sleep, he wondered why Pa and Mr. Hartman didn't seem scared of the Indians they were talking about. *Maybe I'll get braver, too.*

The rain had stopped by the next morning, so the tree-choppers went back to work right after breakfast. After a few hours, they walked ahead to look at the roadway. "Praise the Lord!" Pa said. "Someone has already cleared the next section!"

Because the two wagons made good progress, Pa suggested they should stop an hour early and go hunting. Joshua and Zeke went along, and Zeke turned out to be an excellent hunting dog. He alerted the men to a big raccoon and treed it for them. They also shot four doves. Ma made 'coon stew, and Mrs. Hartman fixed the doves. The families ate together around the fire.

The next day began with a heavy downpour. Streams of muddy water flowed along the wagon ruts. The rain came in sheets and the travelers could barely see the road. Both Pa and Mr. Hartman pulled over to wait. "Even with this rain, we ought to make it to Uniontown today," Pa declared.

When the skies cleared and they got back underway, Pa almost changed his optimistic prediction. A mountain loomed up ahead, and the road became so steep everyone had to get out and walk. Pa led the horses instead of driving the wagon.

"Look, Pa, there's a wrecked wagon!" Joshua pointed to a pile of broken boards and wheels beside a huge rock.

"Th-this must be Ch-chestnut Hill," Mr. Hartman called out from behind them. "M-my brother w-warned me about it. S-said it was s-steep goin' up *and* c-comin' down."

At the summit, the men cut tree brakes and both wagons headed down the steep slope. Halfway down, there was a sickening CRAAACK! The Stewart's wagon lurched backward and scraped to a stop.

"What happened, Pa?" Joshua asked.

"Broken axle is my guess."

"What'll we do now?" Ma moaned.

"We've got a forest full of axles. We'll just cut a new one and fix it."

"C-can I help, M-Mark?" Mr. Hartman asked.

"Thanks, Elijah, but there's no sense in both of us bein' delayed. You go on ahead. We'll look for you in Fort Pitt."

"It's b-been a p-pleasure to t-travel with you and y-your fine f-family. The Lord watch over you."

"Thanks. May the Lord do the same for you." Pa waved to the Hartmans as their wagon carefully edged past.

It took Pa at least five hours to make and fit the new axle. Meanwhile, Ma fixed an early supper for the family. Then they piled back into the repaired wagon.

"Tell us a story, Pa," Beka said.

"This road we're travelin' on is named Braddock's Road, so I'll tell you about General Braddock."

"That big man in Winchester said somethin' about General Braddock," Joshua said.

"Yep. This story starts back when this country was just a collection of British colonies."

"But now we're free from England, right?" Joshua asked.

"Not yet. The colonies signed a declaration of independence about four years ago, but England doesn't want to let us go. Anyway, France built some forts here, too. They claimed part of the riches of this new land," Pa said.

"But what about General Braddock?" Beka asked.

"Twenty-five years ago, England sent him with a large army on ships to Virginia. General Braddock had lots of experience fightin' the British way. His job was to fight the French and their Indian allies. They landed in Alexandria ..."

"That's close to where we lived," Joshua said.

"Right. And General Braddock wanted to go to the same place we're headed."

"Fort Pitt?" Beka asked.

"Yep, except the French who built it named it Fort Doocaine. The general demanded wagons and horses to carry all the supplies and guns his army needed to kick the French out of Fort Doocaine. You *know* how hard it is to go up and down those mountains. He had a tough time, since some of the roads were just trails through the woods."

"So what did he do?" Joshua asked.

"He told the woodsmen to go ahead of the army and chop down the trees so the road would be twelve feet wide." Pa swept his arm from one side of the road to the other.

"That must've been real slow," Joshua said.

"Yep, they took near a month to get almost to the fort."

"*Almost*? Tell us what happened, Pa," Beka said.

"A young feller named George Washington was along as a volunteer, to give advice to General Braddock."

"You mean ... the same one who is leadin' our country *against* the British right now?" Joshua asked.

"Yep, the very same one. He was young, but he knew the Indians would fight by shootin' from behind trees. But General Braddock didn't want to listen to some 'ignorant young colonial' as he called George Washington. He planned to stand his redcoat soldiers in two lines. When the first line fired, they'd step back to reload while the second line fired."

"Sounds pretty good to me," Beka said.

"It did *not* work in the woods against Indians. The general didn't listen to good advice, so he lost the battle, and lost his life, too. He's buried somewhere along this road near Fort Pitt."

"Speaking of Fort Pitt, when will we get there?" Ma asked.

"I can only guess, but maybe another two, three days." Pa scratched his chin as he mentally plotted their course. "We'll follow the Monongahela after Uniontown ..."

"What's a Mong-gong-heala?" Beka asked. "It sounds like a monster."

"Mo-non-ga-hela. It's a river. It winds around and ends up at Fort Pitt. The road follows the river and won't have as many hills and is probably well-traveled."

"I'm sure ready for some easier going," Ma said.

The last two days of travel did prove to be much easier. The road passed through many small settlements. As they neared Fort Pitt, the family noticed more travelers on the road. They even saw some road signs.

Beka said, "Maybe we could stay at an inn and sleep in real beds."

Ma raised her eyebrows. Pa said, "We'll see."

When they were almost to the settlement, Joshua noticed something odd along the river. "Look at those long wooden slides going down to the water. What are they?"

"That's the launchin' dock for a boat company," his father said. "After they build a flatboat, they just slide it right down into the river." The dock swarmed with men. The noise of saws, adzes, and hammers mixed with the shouts of the workers.

"Are we going to buy a flatboat, Pa?" Beka asked.

"Maybe Uncle Philip has already bought us one," Ma said. "Anyway, we're not going to buy one today. I want to get settled somewhere for the night, first."

"Tonight we're stayin' in town." Pa declared.

"Oooh! Can we eat at an inn, too?" Beka asked.

Ma looked surprised but said nothing. Pa smiled and said, "Yep."

"Good. I'm hungry," Joshua said.

The family gawked like sightseers when they first rode into town. "Look at all those stores," Pa said. "Plenty of places in this town to stock up on provisions."

As they continued down the main street Grandma said, "Why, there must be sixty or seventy cabins." Indeed, houses and stores could be seen down every side street.

Pa pulled the wagon to a stop in front of a rambling two-story building showing a pine tree on a weather-beaten sign. Later, around a scarred table in the inn's crowded dining room, Pa reached into his pocket and drew out a worn copy of a handbill advertising flatboats. He read aloud, "Comfortable family boats, well boarded up the sides and roofed to within seven or eight feet of the bow."

"But how much will it cost?" Ma asked.

"It says here, 'sixty cents per foot of length.' We'd want one at least thirty-five feet long."

Ma paused, doing the math in her head. "Mark, we can't afford that. We've got many other things to buy."

"Now, Margaret, you're forgettin' two things. First, we're sharin' the cost with your brother Philip and maybe some other settlers. *And* the Lord says we're to be anxious for nothin'."

"You're right, Mark. I worry too much." Ma hung her head.

"We could pray, couldn't we?" Beka said.

"Let's do that right now." Pa didn't mind being in a crowded room. "Lord, direct us to the boat works that can build us a good strong boat we can afford. And help us to meet up with Philip as planned. And teach Margaret not to worry. Amen."

"Mark, you didn't need to pray that last part," Ma said.

"Oh, no? Then you've learned real fast, I'd say," Pa said. "Now let's get settled for the night. Tomorrow comes early."

Chapter 4

Flatboats
on the Ohio

The noise of horses stomping and wagons creaking and people talking loudly in the inn yard woke everyone early the next day. After breakfast, the whole family climbed into the wagon, eager to buy a flatboat. The first boatbuilding company they stopped at had a hand-lettered sign on the office door.

"NO MORE ORDERS TAKEN UNTIL JUNE 12, 1780."

"A whole month," Ma moaned. "We can't wait that long."

"Don't you fret now, Margaret. We'll just head a ways down River Street here, and try another boatbuildin' establishment." Pa snapped the reins and the horses nickered and headed toward another busy dock area. As they neared, Pa read the weathered sign. "Pennsylvania Boat Works."

"I like the name of this place better anyway," Grandma said.

"Look Pa," Joshua stood up, pointing to the cluster of people standing on the dock. "It looks like Uncle Philip!"

"Sure enough," Pa answered. "Hey, Philip!" he called.

The man turned and waved, then began striding toward them. "Ho there, Stewarts!"

"Philip, we're glad to see you! Been in town long?" Pa asked.

"Got here two days ago. Come see our boat."

"You bought one already?" Pa stood there with his mouth hanging open.

"*We* bought a fine sixty-five foot Kentucky boat, due to be finished tomorrow." Philip beamed as if he'd built it himself. "The *we* includes another family, sharing costs with us."

"Would it hold three more people? We met a fine family as we came up Braddock's Road. They're here in town some-where, lookin' to buy a flatboat, just like us."

Philip grinned. "Of course. Our boat could hold *ten* more people."

"That's good news, and I needed some after a night at the Pine Tree Inn," Ma said.

"It was filthy dirty," Grandma said.

"And noisy," Joshua added.

"A rooster woke me up before it was light," Beka said.

"Why don't we camp out tonight, Margaret?" Pa said.

"Yes, let's do. Where'd you stay, Philip?" she asked.

"We found a private house on the edge of town with a sign up. It wasn't half bad."

"*We*? So you found a bride who'd have you?" Pa had a twinkle in his eye.

"Did Susannah wait for you?" Grandma asked.

"Well, no and yes," Philip said. "She married another fellow, but he died from a fall while buildin' a barn. Susannah was left a widow with a sweet little boy who needed a father. So …"

"So you got two for the price of one," Pa laughed.

"Mark!" Ma put a warning hand on Pa's shoulder. "Philip, we're eager to meet your family. *Our* family will be growing in the near future, too."

"How soon? I mean, when can we expect this blessed event?" Philip asked.

"Early September some time. I'm a little worried about this trip, too," Ma said.

Philip nodded, serious for once. "Flatboat travel does have its hazards." He consulted a scrap of paper from his pocket. "We're travelin' with two other boats, leavin' tomorrow, noon."

"Will the boat be ready by then?" Pa asked.

"Should be."

"How will we know the way?" Ma said.

"That reminds me, I nearly forgot to mention the best part," Philip said. "A tall skinny fellow by the name of Moses Green is goin' along. He's made the trip twice before. He's agreed to pilot all three boats."

"Moses in the Bible led the people to the Promised Land," Grandma observed. Joshua smiled to himself. *Grandma always talks about the Bible.*

Philip laughed, "This Moses is a tough old bird who will lead us safely down the Ohio. "We can begin packin' as soon as the boats are ready tomorrow mornin', and be underway by noon."

"We have plenty more supplies we need to buy," Ma said.

"Right. We'll meet you here tomorrow, first thing," Pa said, shaking hands with Philip. Instead of heading into town, Pa continued down the road beside the river. "Grandma, will you set up camp for us if I give you two good helpers?" Pa gave Ma a knowing smile, then brushed his hand over Joshua's thatch of hair. They parked the wagon on a level spot near the river, under a nice clump of trees, and began unloading kitchen gear, blankets, and food items. Joshua untied the cow and tied her near some tall green grass. Then Ma and Pa drove back to town.

By the time they returned in the late afternoon, much had been accomplished at their campsite. Joshua had gone to get two buckets of water from the river. He and Beka had collected firewood and stones and Joshua made a ring of stones for a fire. Beka had helped Grandma fix a hearty stew and bake some hoecakes. The tantalizing smell of dinner drifted out to greet the returning pair.

"I smell something tasty," Pa called out as he pulled the wagon to a stop.

"Dinner's nearly ready, thanks to these two hard workers," Grandma said.

"Grandma let me make the hoecakes all by myself," Beka said.

"What'd you buy in town, Pa?" Joshua asked. Everyone crowded around the wagon to see.

"There's an adze, an auger, a two-man saw, and a small keg of black powder."

Ma smiled as she showed her choices. "Look at that fine kettle. And the frying pan. It'll hold near two pounds of meat, I figure."

"And I see you got plenty of bacon, salt, and a keg of molasses," Grandma said.

"Yes, and four sacks of corn meal, a …"

"Corn meal! Oh, no!" Grandma waved her hands. "Rebekah, run, get those hoecakes back from the fire before they burn."

The hoecakes were a bit browner than usual, but none were left over. Joshua crumbled his into his stew. Rebekah let Ma split hers and drizzle molasses inside it. After supper, everyone sat around the fire talking. The stars came out. The frogs down by the river tried to outdo each other in a croaking contest. Joshua and Rebekah were glad when it was time for them to snuggle into their blanket-beds in the wagon.

"Will we have any friends our own age when we get to Kentucky?" Beka asked.

"Pa says there are hundreds of settlers goin' down the Ohio these days. Some of them are children, and some of them will be goin' to Limestone."

"I'm excited about going, but I'm scared something bad will happen."

"Go to sleep, Beka. You're a worrier, like Ma." Long after his sister was asleep, Joshua lay there wondering what lay ahead. "I guess I'm a worrier, too," he finally admitted to himself.

In no time at all, it was morning. Joshua and Beka were awake early, too excited to stay asleep. Today they would begin their flatboat journey down the Ohio River. As soon as breakfast was done, they helped pack everything into the wagon again.

On the way to meet Uncle Philip, Pa outlined his plan. "First we empty out the wagon onto the dock, and then I'll take it through the streets and sell it."

"How?" Grandma asked.

"I saw a man ridin' a horse through town yesterday, callin' out for bids. I reckon it'd work for a wagon, too."

"Can I go along, too, Pa?" Joshua asked.

"No, you stay here to help Ma and take care of your sister."

"Aww," Joshua began to grumble. There was so much yet to see in Pittsburgh. As it turned out, the dock area had plenty of excitement. It was the center of activity for all the families who would be going down river with them.

Pa returned in an hour, leading the team. "I got a good price for the wagon. And I saw the Hartmans! They want to go on our flatboat, so they'll be loading up as soon as they finish buyin' supplies." Joshua and Pa spent the rest of the morning carrying their goods into the cabin of the flatboat. The other two flatboats were being loaded nearby.

After Joshua's work was done, he and Beka climbed up the bank to be out of the way. They made a game of guessing what each barrel or bundle contained. "Those four giant barrels have the beef the men were cutting up and salting down this morning. One barrel is for our family."

"I'm glad we get to take our cow Belle with us on the boat." Beka said. "But I wish Pa didn't have to sell the horse before we left," she added wistfully.

"Our saddle horse is safer back in Virginia, Beka. Indians love to steal horses."

Beka's eyes widened. "But Pa is takin' our team to Limestone. What will happen to them?" Joshua immediately wished he'd kept quiet. He hadn't confided his fears to his sister for a good reason. She was already scared of most everything.

"Beka, most of the time, we won't see any Indians in our settlement …"

"But we might see Indians sometime, right?"

"Yes, but probably not in Limestone." This seemed to satisfy her, so Joshua quickly changed the subject. "Look at that pile of fifty pound sacks they're loading. Pa says our sacks of flour and corn meal will have to last till we get our first crop harvested."

"Ma says we'll be planting a garden, too." Beka and her mother had chosen and packaged seeds carefully from last year's harvest to bring along. "What are those funny-shaped bundles?"

"Looks like somebody's kettles and pots, wrapped in blankets and tied with a rope."

"How many people will be on the flatboat with us?" Beka asked. "Besides Uncle Philip and his family, I mean."

"Three Hartmans, and there's Moses Green. He's the tall one with the white beard, and bushy eyebrows. He's the pilot. Then, there's the Washburns—their boy Nathan seems real friendly, even if he does brag a lot. He's the one with the dark curly hair, there, helping the men with that crate."

"How old is he, anyway?"

"Fifteen, he told me."

"Does he have a sister?"

"Yes, *two* sisters. One is a little older than me, the other is about your age, I'd guess."

Beka gave her brother a teasing smile. "Then we'll *both* have girlfriends, won't we.""Not me!" Joshua reddened a bit behind his freckles. *Girls are dumb. And scaredy cats. But Nathan's sister Mary did smile at me when we met this morning.* He quickly changed the subject. "Look, they're loading the animals now. Maybe the people will be next."

"Joshua! Rebekah!" Ma called from the dock. They hurried down. "Here's your lunch." Ma handed them each two hoecakes.

"Are we goin' to leave soon?" Joshua asked between bites.

"Everything is loaded. Most of the people are already on board, too," Ma explained. "Finish your food, then I'll take you to meet your Aunt Susannah and your new cousin." Ma tried in vain to neaten Rebekah's cloud of red-blond curls. "Put your sunbonnet back on, Rebekah. You two be sure to mind your manners, now."

They climbed onto the flat roof of the boat's cabin. Grandma Sarah was talking to their new aunt. Aunt Susannah had lots of curly brown hair piled on top of her head. She smiled a lot, but she was *much* quieter than Uncle Philip was. The two Stewart children liked her right away.

She was busy trying to get her three-year-old son John down from a pile of wooden boxes. He waved impishly at everyone. "John, come down here, right now!" Aunt Susannah was not successful in sounding stern. Joshua and Beka noticed how John completely ignored his mother.

Beka leaned over and whispered to Joshua, "If *we* didn't come when Ma called, we'd get a switching!"

Joshua smiled and nodded at his sister. "Aunt Susannah, I'll get him for you."

"Thank you, Joshua, but then you both might tumble down!" She tried a new command. "John, come down here and meet your new cousins." Soon the little rebel was in the firm grip of his mother.

Pa joined them. "All three boats are loaded."

Moses Green hollered, "Everybody come over here! We're not shovin' off until we have a clear understanding."

There were about fifteen men plus twice as many women and children who finally gathered in a ragged group around their leader. He crossed his arms and set his jaw as he looked from one person to the next. "You've hired me on as your pilot for this trip. I will get you safely to Limestone and Ruddell's station. But get this straight. What I say is law. We start when I say, and put to shore when I say."

Many of the men nodded in agreement. After a pause, the stern-faced pilot continued, "At times we'll have to lash the three boats together, whenever the current is treacherous. Men, keep your rifles at hand, loaded and primed. But don't go shooting Indians just for sport. We shove off shortly. Any questions?"

One man shouted, "Kentucky, here we come!" Others joined in, cheering. Two men shot their rifles into the air.

"Shove off!" Moses Green yelled. Everyone scrambled onto the flatboats. The pilot and Mr. Hartman used long poles to push the awkward flatboat away from the shore. Pa and Uncle Philip manned the two oars at the front of the boat as it glided to the center of the river. The other two boats followed.

"It's hard to believe we're finally on our way to Limestone," Ma said.

Grandma said, "Let's call this boat Noah's Ark."

"Why, Grandma?" Beka asked. "There's no flood."

"And the pilot's name is Moses, not Noah," Joshua added.

"Because it's got more animals than people," Grandma said.

Joshua nodded and pointed toward the pen at the back of the boat. "I counted two horses, three cows, ten chickens in cages, two pigs, and four dogs."

Nathan Washburn and his sisters joined them. "That's my pa on the steerin' oar in the back, talking to Moses Green," Nathan pointed. "My pa is helpin' him pilot this boat."

Joshua nodded toward the two men on the oars. "There's our pa and our Uncle Philip."

Beka smiled shyly at Nathan's two sisters. "My name's Rebekah."

Mary tossed her head and her black hair rippled. "My name's Mary, and this is my sister Hannah." She gave a little curtsey. "May as well get acquainted. Ma says it'll be six or seven days till we hit Limestone."

Hannah's dark brown hair was braided and peeked out from under her sunbonnet on each side. The three girls were soon chatting as if they had been friends for years.

"You must be from the South. You talk funny," Mary said.

"Yes, we're from Virginia. You talk funny too. Where do you hail from?"

"Pennsylvania," Hannah said, giggling.

"Are you going to Limestone?" Beka asked.

"Yep. Everybody on this boat is headed there," Mary said.

They watched the scenery gliding past them on both sides. The busy dock area gave way to more of Pittsburgh's cabins. "Those cabins are so close together, why you could spit from one to the next," Nathan said.

Pa joined them. "Seem mighty crowded, don't they. Now, where we're goin', the cabins won't even be within sight of each other." He smiled as if this suited him just fine. A little farther on, Pa pointed to a large log structure. Its angled log walls had towers at each corner. "That's Fort Pitt. The whole town goes inside the fort when there's an Indian raid or an attack by the British."

Small groups of soldiers and Indians walked toward the fort as the flatboat floated past. "Look, there's some Indians right now," Joshua said.

"Right here in Pittsburgh?" Beka asked.

Pa laughed. "They are probably visitin' the fort's trading post. And probably not out lookin' for any trouble," he said.

Moses Green shouted for them to look up ahead. "This point of land is called the Gateway to the West. It's where the Ohio begins." Ahead they could see a sparkling river joining the muddy Monongahela.

Pa exclaimed, "It's a beautiful river, I'd say!"

Moses Green nodded in agreement, then said, "Beautiful and dangerous."

Chapter 5

Uncle Philip's Stories

As they continued down the Ohio, the travelers saw fewer and fewer signs of civilization. Trees crowded both banks. The oarsmen worked to keep the flatboats in the center of the river, away from dangers near the shore.

Moses Green yelled to Joshua and Nathan, "Ho, you boys, come here!" They hurried to where he stood, wondering if they had done something wrong. "Listen, in the days ahead there may be submerged trees in the water to sink this boat. You boys watch for 'em and holler if you see any." Nathan and Joshua nodded and clambered to the front of the boat. They liked this job, since they were busy watching everything anyway.

"Look," Joshua pointed toward shore. A break in the trees showed a neat little cabin behind a split-rail fence.

"That's just like the cabin I want when we get to Limestone," Nathan said.

"And look at the apple trees beside the house—I wonder if there'll be any of those in Limestone?" The scent of the blossoms drifted across the water. As they turned to look out for trees in the river, Joshua's heart started pounding. A huge tree blocked the river ahead.

They both turned and began shouting, "Watch out! A big tree in the water!"

The men grabbed the heavy poles and began pushing the boat toward the left side. William Washburn, at the steering oar, guided the flatboat through the narrow opening. "I hope we don't get hung up on the shore," Pa grunted as he pushed against the pole, guiding the boat perilously close to the bank.

"Stand back!" Uncle Philip shouted. Nathan, Joshua, and the girls scrambled away from the edge of the roof. The branches of the tree scraped the side of the boat.

Suddenly a large branch whipped back across the roof, knocking Mary into the water.

"Help! Somebody, help!" she screamed.

"Grab hold of the branches, Mary!" Joshua shouted. "Nathan, can you swim?"

Nathan shook his head in fear and ran to get help.

Hannah and Beka began to cry. Mary struggled to hold onto the branches and keep her head above water. The current was tugging at her, trying to sweep her away.

"Pa, come quick!" Joshua shouted. Pa and William Washburn ran to the side of the boat.

Mr. Washburn cried, "I can't swim! Somebody save Mary!"

Pa climbed over the side and swam over to the struggling girl. Mary grabbed onto her rescuer and held on for dear life.

"Let me loose, Mary!" Pa said. "Let me pull *you* back to the boat."

Many hands reached down to pull the bedraggled Mary back on board. Her father hugged her and turned to Pa. "Thanks for savin' my girl!"

Mary's dress was torn and her black hair was tangled and matted, but she managed a wry smile. "I told my friends I was going down the Ohio … I guess I should've said down *into* it."

Moses Green clapped Pa on the back. "Good work, Stewart." He turned and spoke to the rest of the men, "Now, let's get this boat back into the center of the river."

Later that day, Nathan said, "Look, Joshua!" There were five deer pausing to drink at the river's edge. They stared at the flatboats for a few moments, and then raised their white tails as they bounded back into the woods. Nathan let out a low whistle. "If I had my gun with me, I could've bagged a deer for our supper."

"You've got your own gun?" Joshua asked.

"Yes, but Pa made me stow it. Maybe when we see some Indians, he'll let me get it out."

"I'd like to have a gun to go huntin' with, but shooting Indians …" Joshua let his voice trail off. It made him uncomfortable to think about killing a living, breathing *person*. And yet he had heard Uncle Philip tell about Indians killing settlers. He'd have to ask Pa what he thought about it.

"Well, *I* can't wait to kill me some Indians," Nathan boasted. "They're nothin' but savages, anyway."

"What's that near the shore?" Mary asked, pointing to a tangle of boards and branches.

"Looks like it *used* to be a flatboat," Nathan answered.

"I hope our flatboat doesn't end up like that." Joshua shuddered as they passed by the wreck. *I wonder if anyone drowned.*

"I hope that bossy old Moses Green is as good a pilot as he says he is," Nathan said. It was the first, but not the last wreck they saw on their journey.

They saw few other man-made things on shore—a rare settlement, a cabin off in the woods. Mostly they saw trees. Hundreds of squirrels scurried up and down and between the trees. The sound of their chattering could be heard clearly across the water. Zeke pricked up his ears and watched their antics with interest.

Beka saw Ma and the other women climbing down the ladder into the cabin, so she and the girls followed. The cabin of the flatboat was packed with boxes, bundles, barrels, sacks, and various large tools and took up most of the sixty-foot length of their "Kentucky boat." In one corner was a large open box filled with sand. This would be their "stove" for the journey. A pipe ran from the stove out through the roof of the flatboat.

Aunt Susannah was slicing salt pork into a large frying pan. Ma mixed dough for biscuits. Hettie Washburn was peeling and cutting up potatoes. The girls were put to work making the meal for the seventeen passengers.

When everything was cooked, the girls carried it up to the others on the roof. Joshua and Nathan were almost too busy listening to Uncle Philip to stop and eat. Philip, however, was ready for dinner. "Thank you, girls," he boomed. "I'm hungry enough to eat a bear!" He took the bowl of food and continued, "Come join us!" The girls hurried to get their own dinners and soon were perched beside their brothers on the cabin roof.

"Uncle Philip, tell us more frontier stories," Joshua said.

"Tell us one about Indians," said Nathan.

Uncle Philip laughed and waved his arm at the river before them. "Last time I floated down the Ohio, we had a real close encounter with some Indians."

"A ... lot of them?" Beka asked.

"Yep, lots of 'em!"

"Were you on a flatboat?" Mary asked.

"Yep, a Kentucky boat, same as this one."

Uncle Philip took a few bites of his dinner and began his story. "Well, it's a beautiful day, we're floatin' along, mindin' our own business. We see this man on the shore. He's beggin' us and yellin' '*Help! Help!*' His shirt's torn, and he's bleedin'. The first boat—I was in the second—goes in real close to shore to help the man. Some of us holler, 'It's a trick! It's a trick!' That first boat finally turns and heads back toward the middle of the river. Just then, maybe two dozen savages jump out from the woods. Their faces, chests, and arms are painted up somethin' awful. They drag four canoes out of the bushes, and give chase! Now flatboats ain't built for speed, so we just know we got a fight on our hands." Uncle Philip paused and smiled, then calmly ate some more of his dinner.

Nathan obviously wished he'd been along on that trip. "Did you get to shoot any Indians?"

"Well, I was just gettin' to that part," Uncle Philip laughed. "Our boat is a ways behind, so we can't get a good shot. But maybe we don't want to get any closer. I guess we're kinda attached to our scalps!"

Joshua gulped and reached up to feel his thatch of hair. "What happened next? Did both boats get away?"

"Well, the men on the first flatboat, they wait till the first canoe load of Indians comes real close, then they take aim and let loose a volley! Only two Indians are hit, and all four canoes just keep coming! The Indians are shootin', too, and a few of the settlers are hit. They're reloadin' so fast you'd think they're in a contest," Philip laughed. "The next volley from the settlers takes out a few more from the first canoe. But the Indians just keep on comin'! So now *our* flatboat is close enough and we're gettin' in some good shots, and even more Indians are gettin' hit!"

"Serves 'em right!" Nathan hooted.

"Finally the Indians turn those canoes around and paddle right back to shore. Probably they'll try the same trick on the next flatboat that comes along."

"Do you suppose there'll be Indians tryin' that trick on us, Uncle Philip?" Joshua had a prickly feeling all down his back as he envisioned Indians attacking *their* flatboat.

"Maybe so! But Moses Green won't fall for it! We'll stay in the middle of the river and be plenty safe!"

Mary and Beka stared out over the water, thinking of canoes full of Indians. Suddenly they caught a movement—a dark shape in the trees near the shore.

"Look," Mary said. "Over beyond that big tree … I think it's a bear!"

"Yes, I see it too!" Nathan called out.

Their voices must have carried across the water to the bear. It stood on its back legs, glanced in their direction, and then lumbered off into the woods.

"Where? I didn't get to see it!" Hannah said.

"Don't you worry, Miss Hannah. Where you're goin', you'll see plenty of bears," Uncle Philip laughed. "That reminds me of a story."

"Tell us," Joshua said.

"Please?" begged the others.

"How about another bowl of meat and potatoes first?"

"I'll get it," Beka volunteered. As soon as she returned with it, Philip took a few bites and launched into the story.

"Well, these two brothers 're out huntin' with their dog. They're about the age of you two boys, I'd guess. They have only one gun between them, though. They spot a bear and the younger boy decides to shoot it." Uncle Philip hunched down and aimed an imaginary gun at a spot on shore. "He creeps up close, aims, and fires. That bear is wounded just enough to be fightin' mad. Their dog is barkin' and barkin' at the bear, which is the only thing keepin' that wounded bear away from the boys."

"I'm gonna get a huntin' dog when we get to Limestone," Nathan bragged.

Uncle Philip nodded, took a few more bites, and continued. "The boy with the gun runs behind a tree and reloads his rifle for a second shot. He shoots *again* and misses the bear's head, but gets his paw." Uncle Philip held up his hand and pointed to the middle of his palm. "This time the bear runs away and jumps into a creek. The dumb dog chases the bear, and then jumps in after him! The bear grabs the dog. The boys come along and try a third shot at the bear, to save their dog. The boy aims, fires, and click!" He flung his arm in a wide arc. "The flint flies off!"

"What's a flint, Uncle Philip?" asked Beka.

Nathan broke in, "That's the part of the gun that makes a spark to burn the powder that shoots the bullet."

"Oh." Beka half understood this explanation.

"What happened to the dog?" Joshua reached down to pat Zeke's head.

"Well, when a dog fights a bear, it's 'most always the bear that wins," Uncle Philip chuckled. "So the younger boy gets out his knife and starts to jump into the creek to rescue his dog. His big brother stops him. But the poor dog is thrashin' around in the water and yelpin' for all he's worth."

"Poor dog!" Hannah said.

"Both those boys get on hands and knees and hunt like mad for that missin' flint. Sure enough, they find it and put it back in the gun. Now they try one more time to shoot that bear."

"Did they hit it?" Beka was secretly pulling for the bear.

"Did they save the dog?" Hannah asked.

"Yes to both questions! They not only hit that bear, they kill it! But I bet you can't guess what they did next!"

"Skin it?" Nathan said.

"Nope. Good guess, but skinnin' a bear is too big a job for two boys. They had to go get some help. But first they find a strong saplin', and tie a rope to it so they can bend it way over. Then they tie the bear's leg to the other end of the rope. When they let go, WHUP! Up goes that bear into the air, hangin' out of reach of the wolves. The next day, their pa and his friends come and drag that bear back to their cabin. It's fall, and that fat bear has lots of meat and grease for cookin' all winter long."

"I'm going to shoot me a bear when we get to Limestone," Nathan said.

"No doubt," Uncle Philip chuckled.

And lots of Indians, too, thought Joshua.

Uncle Philip left to take his turn at the steering oar.

No one spoke for a long while after that. They listened to the quiet slap of the oars in the water. The shadows length-ened and the mists began to rise along the shore. *I know it's just my imagination, but it looks like two Indians crouched by that clump of trees ahead,* Joshua thought.

When it was nearly dark, Moses Green called out from the pilot boat, "Pull to shore." The sound echoed from the banks on the opposite shore. As the flatboats glided to a stop, one man from each craft hopped out and tied them to trees.

Moses Green walked back along the shore. "All you men meet by the first boat in two minutes." The group quickly assembled. "We're heading into dangerous territory," the pilot began. "Your life may depend on followin' my orders, so listen carefully. We must stay together, both on the water and as we camp each night. Keep a sharp eye on what's goin' on around you. Indians often travel in small huntin' parties, anywhere from three to ten or twelve. That means they won't generally attack a well-armed group like ours. Keep your guns primed and close at hand."

Nathan leaned over and asked his pa, "Can we get my gun out now, Pa?"

"Maybe."

The lanky pilot continued, "We will take turns standing watch each night. First three hours, you, Washburn. Next three, Hartman. Last three, Stewart. Thanks, men. See you all in the mornin'."

Joshua was glad that someone would be guarding them during the night. *I've heard so much about Indians today, I don't know if I can even go to sleep,* Joshua thought. Some people planned to sleep on shore. Others preferred to find a spot on the cabin roof.

"Pa, I'd feel safer on the boat," Joshua said. Ma, Beka, and Grandma Sarah agreed. As they settled down for the night, Joshua asked his father a question he had been troubled about most of the day. "Pa, do you think it's right to kill Indians?"

Pa didn't answer right away. He stared into the shadowy darkness on shore, as if he might see a Shawnee war party. "Well, son," he said slowly, "if I had to protect you and Rebekah, Ma, and Grandma Sarah from being scalped, you can be sure that I'd shoot to kill."

Joshua gulped at the awful picture that Pa's words brought to his mind. "Well, Nathan has his own gun, and he says he can't *wait* to kill his first Indian."

Again, Pa paused a long while before answering. "The Bible teaches us we ought to live at peace with all men, if it's possible, son. God made the white man *and* the red man. Never let hatred take over your heart."

Joshua lay awake thinking about what Pa had said. The stars came out one by one. The river slapped gently against the boat. On shore, a chorus of night sounds was led by the "skree-kick, skree-kick" of crickets. Deep in the woods, a screech owl's trembling wail floated in the air, then faded. Moments later, the owl's mate sent back an answering call. *Maybe there are Indians listenin' to these same sounds,* Joshua thought. *Do Indians* have *to be our enemies? Isn't there enough land for everyone?*

Chapter 6

A Map of
the Trip

Joshua awakened to the smell of coffee. Beka was shaking his shoulder. "Hey, are you going to sleep all day?" It took him a moment to remember where he was … on the roof of a flatboat, partway down the Ohio River to a new home in Kentucky country.

"What's for breakfast?" he asked.

Beka grinned as if she had privileged information. "Ma fixed a kettle of mush and molasses. But you really should ask me what's for *supper*!"

"All right, Beka. What's for supper?"

"Maybe roast pigeon. Pa and Uncle Philip went out to see if they could shoot a few birds or something for us."

"Awww …" Joshua made a face. "They shoulda woke me up!"

"Why would they want you along? You don't have a gun. You would just scare the birds away."

"Go 'way! I need to get ready for breakfast." He climbed off the boat and walked down to the water.

As Joshua washed his face in the river, he noticed the thick fog hanging over the water. Behind him, the woods had only a few wisps of fog. *Good thing, too, or else Pa and Uncle Philip couldn't see to hunt …* Just then, two shots, one right after the other, split the silence. Then several more shots rang out. Joshua hurried up the bank to get his breakfast. Ma stirred a kettle held over a small fire by two forked sticks.

"Good morning, young man." Grandma sat on a blanket with the Bible in her lap. She patted a spot beside her. "Bring your breakfast here and I'll give you a bit of the Word to go with it."

"Can I come, too?" Beka plopped down next to Grandma without waiting for an answer. Joshua got his breakfast and leaned against a nearby tree.

"Here's your verse from your own book, Joshua. Joshua 1:9 says, 'Have I not commanded thee? Be strong and of a good courage. Be not afraid, neither be thou dismayed: for the Lord thy God is with thee whithersoever thou goest.'"

Beka asked, "What's whithersoever mean?" Joshua was glad she'd asked—he wasn't so sure himself.

"That's *anywhere*," Grandma explained. "Anywhere we go, God says He is with us."

Beka's voice quavered a bit. "Even Indian country?"

His sister's question mirrored Joshua's own unspoken one.

"*Especially* Indian country, Rebekah." Grandma hugged her to emphasize her words. "It's often when we're in danger that we learn our best lessons in trusting the Lord."

"Uncle Philip told us some scary stories yesterday on the boat," Joshua began. "So now I have this awful feeling the Indians are out to *get* us!"

"Then this verse will help you to be brave." Grandma read it over several more times for them. "And Joshua, you remember that I've prayed that you will be a brave leader for our family."

Joshua didn't feel brave at all. Each mile they had traveled down this wide and beautiful river, he had felt an ever-stronger sense of danger. "Pray again, Grandma," he said. As she prayed, Joshua prayed too. *Help me not to be afraid, God, because you've promised to be with me.* As he finished praying, the knot of fear eased a little.

"Joshua!" Nathan came bounding past. "My pa says it's nearly time to shove off!" He was gone before Joshua could answer. Nathan continued down the line of breakfast fires until everyone had been informed. All along the shore, women packed up blankets and pots.

"Will you two please help?" Ma asked. "Joshua, take the kettle back to the boat, and Rebekah, douse the fire." Splash! The fire hissed and smoke rose up among the trees.

"What's that?" Beka asked, pointing toward the river. Joshua and Beka raced to the water's edge and strained to see what it was. Like a dream floating back into memory, a long flatboat slowly emerged from the fog.

A deep voice hallooed across the water. "Whooooose boats? Whoooooo's the pilot?"

Moses Green stood and called out the answer, then shouted a question of his own. "Wheeere you boooound?"

"Boonesboro." The answer echoed several times across the fog-shrouded water.

"Hmm, I wonder where that is," said Joshua. "I wish we had a map."

Beka said, "Let's make one."

"How?"

"I don't know …"

"Shove off!" shouted Moses Green. Everyone scrambled to get aboard. After much pushing and grunting by the men working the poles, the three flatboats glided into the center current of the Ohio. Fog hovered over the water and swirled lazily as the vessels slid through.

Beka tugged on her brother's sleeve. "Let's figure out how to make a map, Joshua."

"Uncle Philip will help us." Joshua headed to the side where his uncle manned an oar.

Uncle Philip smiled broadly when he heard their idea. "You two are real adventurers. Just how much territory are you goin' to include in your cartography?" He laughed again as they puzzled over the unfamiliar word.

"Cartog-what?" Beka asked.

"Cartography. That's just a fancy word for map makin'."

"Let's make it from where we lived in Virginia to Limestone, in Kentucky country," said Joshua.

"You'll need a big piece of paper, then," Uncle Philip chuckled.

Beka had already thought about this problem. "Ma's been saving flour sacks. Maybe we could use one of them."

"That would be better than paper." Joshua was genuinely surprised when his sister came up with such a good idea.

"Joshua, work this oar for a minute," Uncle Philip directed. "I'll get my quill pen and a bottle of ink from below. Beka, you see if your ma will part with a flour sack."

Before long, they both returned with the needed supplies. Nathan and his sisters wandered over to see what was happening.

"Hey, what are you going to do with that sack?" Mary asked.

Joshua smiled, glad that they had come. "My uncle is helping us make a map."

"I've made maps before. Let me help," Nathan said.

Uncle Philip laughed, "You can all help."

Uncle Philip used his knife to cut down the sides of the flour sack, spreading it out in front of them. He drew in the Chesapeake Bay, marking a squiggly shoreline. He drew the roughly triangular shape of their home state. "There's Virginia. Put an X for Woodbridge, Joshua, right here."

"Where's Pennsylvania?" Mary asked.

"Not so fast!" Uncle Philip said. "You surely want me to draw *Mary*land!" He laughed as he drew the border for that state. "You can mark Cumberland right here, Mary." When she finished, he took the pen and began to draw again. "Now, here's the *long* state of Pennsylvania, and here is Braddock's Road."

"That has lots of mountains!" Joshua added. "We counted at least ten."

"I want to draw the biggest one, where our axle broke," Beka said.

"Chestnut Ridge," Joshua prompted.

"Draw that right here, Rebekah, and put Uniontown beside it. Then I'll draw the rest of Braddock's Road."

"Let me draw something, too," Nathan said.

"You can mark Fort Pitt." Uncle Philip pointed to a spot and Nathan put an X and labeled it.

"We're from Beaver, and it's right near Fort Pitt." Nathan drew that in, too.

"Can I draw something, too?" Hannah asked.

"You could put in some of the Ohio River, starting right here at Fort Pitt," Uncle Philip offered.

Pa hurried up to them. "Sorry to interrupt geography class, but it looks like trouble ahead." The river had narrowed into two channels as it flowed around a large island directly ahead. Steep banks made the water choppy. Beyond the island, the river seemed to disappear as it made a sharp bend.

"Steer toward the right-hand channel!" Moses Green yelled.

Thud! Suddenly the boat lurched. Joshua nearly slipped overboard. "What happened, Pa?" he shouted.

"We ran aground! The current pushed us into the shallow water near the island." Pa and two other men picked up the long poles and began to push. Nothing moved. The boat was stuck fast.

"We need to lighten the load!" Moses Green yelled. "Everyone off except two women and you two boys." He pointed to Joshua and Nathan. "You push with the poles while we push the boat from the side."

"That may work. Let's try it." Pa jumped into the shallow water near the shore. The rest of the men were close behind. The women and children seemed to take forever to get off.

"Shove hard on the count of three," Moses Green said. "And you on the poles, push as hard as you can! One … two … *three!*" As everyone strained, the boat moved several inches, then stopped.

Joshua, panting, leaned to look over the side. "Let's try again!"

"This big boat is stuck for sure," Nathan said, tossing down his pole.

"You boys get back to pushing!" Moses Green yelled at them. Joshua and Aunt Susanna pushed with one pole; Nathan and his ma used the other.

"Now! One … two … *three!*" Everyone pushed with all his might. Slowly the boat inched back toward the river and finally floated free.

"Hooray!" Mary, Hannah, and Beka led the cheers of the ones on the shore.

"Climb back on. We need to get movin'," Moses Green called out.

The rest of the day went much more smoothly. Just when Joshua began to get very hungry, the three boats tied up on an island for supper. "C'mon, Joshua. The men are going to collect some firewood," Pa said, shouldering his rifle. "Maybe we'll find us a deer for supper, too." Nathan, his pa and three other men headed into the woods.

"Stay close to camp, men," Moses Green said.

Joshua enjoyed walking in the woods. "When we get to Limestone, will you teach me how to shoot, Pa?"

"We'll have to get you your own rifle."

"Yes! Then I could help you hunt."

"And help me defend our cabin …"

"Against wolves?"

"And anythin' or anyone else that might attack."

The idea that he might have to shoot an Indian still bothered Joshua, but he quickly put it out of his mind. "Thanks, Pa. I can't wait to have a gun like Nathan."

The hunting trip didn't produce a deer, but there was plenty of smaller game for supper. Joshua was in charge of roasting the pigeons. "Keep them turning slowly over the coals, now, Joshua," Grandma said. Beka came up with an armload of firewood.

"Don't put any more wood on now, silly! You'll burn our dinner."

"You always get the fun jobs!" Beka stomped off to help Ma with the biscuits. Grandma fixed coffee. By the time they all sat down to eat, Joshua was really hungry. Everything tasted delicious.

Before they shoved off again, Moses Green called a meeting. Joshua wondered what he had to tell them. Everyone from all three boats gathered to listen.

"As we travel further down the Ohio, we're more likely to see Indians," the pilot warned. "They'll generally leave us alone as long as we leave them alone."

Nathan leaned over to whisper to Joshua, "I'm not goin' to miss my chance to shoot an Indian, though."

Joshua frowned at Nathan. "You'll get us all into trouble."

Moses Green continued. "Tomorrow we reach the mouth of the Great Kanawha River. We'll stop at the trading post there."

Joshua's heart jumped. He looked at Pa with the unspoken question, "Can we buy my gun?" written all over his face. Pa smiled and nodded. Joshua closed his eyes and imagined how he would shoot a bear and rescue Beka.

Moses Green's voice broke into his thoughts. "We shove off in ten minutes. We can get three more hours' travel before nightfall."

The clear water sparkled and rippled in the rays of the late afternoon sun. *What a peaceful scene!* Nathan and his sisters came to sit with Joshua and Beka. Joshua quickly looked away, embarrassed, when he caught Mary looking at him. Mr. Hartman sang in a strong clear voice and soon everyone joined in. *The echoes from the banks make it sound a bit spooky,* Joshua thought. One new chorus really caught his imagination.

"'Tis I can delve and plow, love,
And you can spin and sew,
And we'll settle on the banks
Of the pleasant Ohio."

*We really **are** going to have our own farm on the banks of the Ohio!*

Chapter 7

An Unexpected Journey

Today was the sixth day of their trip on "Noah's Ark." Three days ago, they had stopped at a trading post for supplies, including a new rifle for Joshua. Mornings were now a routine— breakfast, cleanup, then Moses Green's call, "Shove off!"

As they poled to the center to begin the day's journey, Joshua perched near Pa. "I want to get some practice with my new rifle, Pa."

"I can teach you how to load it right now. Go get it from below."

Joshua needed no second invitation and returned quickly with the gun, a small Kentucky rifle.

"Hand me the powder horn," Pa said. "This little horn attached to the big one is for measurin' the black powder charge."

"Let me pour it in."

"Good, now wrap this lead ball in this greased patch of fabric … next take the ramrod … push it all the way down the barrel."

Joshua smiled as he completed each task. "That's done. Now what's next?"

"Look … this little dish with a metal lid on it built into the base of the barrel … it's called the primin' pan," Pa explained. "It holds a fine kind of black powder that ignites easily when the spark from the flint hits it."

"Oh, and the flame goes through that little hole beside the pan?"

"Yep. Then the big charge of black powder explodes and shoots the ball wherever you're aimin'."

Joshua held the gun in shooting position. It wobbled, in spite of all his efforts.

"Hold 'er steady, there."

"I'm going to need lots of practice before I can hit anythin' with this!" Joshua exclaimed.

Uncle Philip joined them, laughing. "Watch out, all you wolves and bears! The mighty hunter is here with his new rifle."

Pa asked Uncle Philip, "Shall we take him out huntin' when we stop for supper?"

"Fine idea." He turned to Joshua, "Meanwhile, let's add more to that map of yours."

They unrolled the map and inked in the rest of the Ohio River all the way to Limestone. Uncle Philip marked in the largest Shawnee village, Chillicothe. Joshua practiced several times how to say it: chill-a-coth-ee.

Nathan came along and admired the finished product. "Wanta play Mumble-the-Peg?"

"Sure, but what *is* it?"

"C'mon, I'll show ya." The boys found a space on the roof of the boat cabin and scratched a large circle. "Toss your knife up, then the one who gets it closest to this mark …" Nathan made an X, and then demonstrated with a deft toss. Joshua tried his hand at it and found it wasn't as easy as Nathan made it look.

"Hey, that looks like fun," Mary said, as she and the other girls joined them. "That was a good toss, Joshua."

"Stand back, girls," Nathan warned. "Let's play the game now—you can go first, Joshua." Nathan won most of the time at first. After a while, Joshua acquired the knack of tossing his knife so it landed just where he wanted. Whenever his toss landed closer to the mark than Nathan's, the girls cheered for him.

After a while, Mary asked, "Can we play this time?"

"No! You'd get hurt. Just go away. All of you!" Nathan pushed his sister to emphasize his demand.

Just then, Moses Green walked past. "What's goin' on here?" he asked.

"Nothin'," Nathan said, quickly hiding the knife.

"I warn't born yesterday," Moses Green said, glancing at the circle the boys had drawn. "You're a danger to the other passengers, throwin' knives around like that. If I see those knives even one more time, they'll be at the bottom of the river!" He turned on his heel and strode back to the steering oar.

Nathan scowled. "He'd better not try to take *my* knife!"

"That's not fair. We weren't hurtin' anybody." Joshua turned and nearly ran into Pa, who had seen the whole incident.

"Look there, Joshua." Pa pointed to the dense under-growth on shore. "This country is *wild!* Never saw jungle like that in Virginia."

Joshua smiled in spite of himself. Pa always tried to cheer him up. "Yes, Pa. And we never had trees this big in Virginia, neither."

"Right. This wild country is all new to us. Moses Green's job is to keep us alive." Pa gave Joshua a stern look, but said nothing more.

Near the end of the day, Uncle Philip called, "Hey, look up there!" He pointed to a high cliff above the river. "They call that Hangin' Rock." There, silhouetted against the sky, stood an Indian. He was obviously watching the flatboats making their way down river. Joshua shuddered.

Mr. Washburn called, "Let's see who can shoot that Indian." He grabbed his rifle and took aim.

"Anybody who shoots gets tossed into the river!" Moses Green said.

Nathan's pa muttered something under his breath, but put his gun down. Pa leaned over to Joshua and said, "I hope he's learned a lesson, one we'd all better learn. What Moses Green says is law on this boat." Joshua knew Pa's words were meant especially for him.

Later, just as they began to angle the boat to shore for supper, Joshua shouted for Nathan. "Look at that giant tree!"

"Whoo-ee!" Nathan whistled. "I wonder if it's hollow."

"Maybe—then it would make a great hideout. It must be thirty feet around."

Nathan thought a while, and then exclaimed, "Let's measure it."

"How?'

"We can use a rope … my pa's got a ten foot rope."

"That tree is bigger around than that," Joshua said.

"We can use it anyway; I know a way. C'mon, let's get it from the cabin so we'll be ready when we land."

"We'd better wait till after we eat, and get your pa and mine to go along."

"You know they'll say 'no.' Besides, it's so close to where we're stoppin', we'll be back before they even miss us." Nathan climbed down the ladder and soon returned with the rope.

"What if someone sees that and asks …"

"Quit worryin'." Nathan quickly hid the rope behind a box on the cabin roof. "As soon as everyone is busy tyin' up and unloadin', we'll just slip away …"

"But Moses Green said …"

"I don't care what that old windbag said!" As soon as they landed, Nathan slipped the rope out of its hiding place and climbed onto shore. Joshua hung back. "Come on, Joshua."

"Pa and Uncle Philip were gonna take me out with my new gun …"

"The tree is just up the river a little way. We'll be back before anyone notices we're gone." The boys hurried upriver to find "their tree." It took them longer to reach it than they had expected.

Joshua leaned back to look up. "What a tree. I can't even see the top."

Nathan took his knife and slashed a mark on the tree. He handed one end of the rope to Joshua. "Take this as far as it will go and make another slash."

"Do you think this tree is more than thirty feet around?"

"Maybe forty," Nathan said.

"I wonder how old it is."

"At least a hundred years." Nathan counted the slashes and completed the measurement. "There. It's about thirty-three feet around." Nathan began looping the rope neatly.

"Let's head back. We'd better hurry or they'll think we've been scalped," he said.

"Scalped." Joshua gulped, then smiled and repeated under his breath, "Be not afraid ... God is with thee ... whithersoever thou goest ... now what was the rest of that verse?" Suddenly he caught a movement out of the corner of his eye. "Hey! Look out!" Joshua's heart stopped beating as his worst fears came to life. Seven Shawnee Indians with painted faces jumped from the underbrush. They grabbed the boys, who struggled wildly. Neither one had a chance to escape.

Nathan began shouting, but an Indian quickly clamped a strong hand over his mouth. "You yell, we kill," the leader growled at them. One Indian bound Joshua's wrists behind his back. The same thing happened to Nathan. Then the Shawnees fastened rawhide leashes around their necks. Joshua felt limp with fear; his legs almost buckled under him.

One of the Shawnees was about Nathan's age. His braided scalp lock was decorated with beads and feathers. A jagged scar across his nose gave him an extra fierceness. He glared at the captured boys and spat in their faces. He shouted a stream of angry words in Shawnee and pulled out his tomahawk. *He's going to kill us right now! Lord, please help us.*

The lead Shawnee grabbed the threatening arm of the younger Indian, and hissed "Peshewa!" Then to the others he said, "Wehpetheh!" At this signal, the Indians yanked the leashes to hurry their captives along the trail through the woods.

Oh, I wish I'd listened to Moses Green ... I wish I'd listened to my pa! Where are they taking us? What will Ma and Pa do? I didn't even tell them we were going to measure that tree. Will I ever see them again? Should we try to escape? Anguished questions swirled around in Joshua's mind like eddies around the oars of their flatboat. Then he remembered ... *the Lord thy God is with thee whithersoever thou goest.* This thought alone kept him from breaking down as he stumbled along, farther and farther away from Ma and Pa and the rest of those he loved.

The forest trail they rushed along suddenly opened to a grassy clearing. Nine horses, two packed with bedrolls and supplies, had been staked to graze. The Indians quickly mounted their horses. The leader of the Indians untied the boys' wrists and motioned to them to climb on a horse behind a Shawnee brave. *I'm glad it's not that one who spit in our faces,* Joshua thought. The Indian tied Joshua's rawhide leash to his waist. *No chance to slide off and escape. I wonder if anyone will be following our trail. Just a few minutes ago, we were measuring that tree.*

The trail paralleled the river for about a mile, and then led to the water's edge. The lead Shawnee kneed his horse ahead into the water. The other horses plunged in behind and began swimming to the other side. The trail immediately disappeared into dense underbrush.

Joshua tried to notice any landmarks as the horses made their way along the trail. *We're following this stream away from the Ohio ... let's see, the sun is coming through the trees a little to my left ... we must be going northwest. We're heading into Indian country.*

Joshua could sometimes glimpse Nathan ahead of him through the trees as the path turned to the left or right. *I wonder if Nathan's planning to escape. We'd better watch out for the one called Peshewa, that angry one with the crooked nose.*

Many hours later, when it was fully dark, they stopped to make camp for the night. The boys' wrists were again tied behind their backs. The lead Shawnee, who was called Wasegoboah by the others, pointed to Joshua and Nathan and gave commands to the others. One Shawnee threw them some pieces of dried meat. The boys just sat for a minute, wondering what to do.

Peshewa came over to watch. "Eat!" he shouted. Joshua leaned over to eat the food, and Peshewa kicked it away, laughing. The others laughed too, except Wasegoboah. He came over with a gourd of water from the stream and gave each boy a long drink. He also put a handful of dried corn into their mouths. *I'm not very hungry, but I need to keep up my strength. Maybe tonight we can escape.*

All thoughts of escape died as the boys watched their captors pound stakes into the ground. Joshua and Nathan's hands and feet were securely tethered to the stakes with rawhide strips. Peshewa came over to spit in their faces again and kicked them each a few times. Wasegoboah spoke some warning words, and the angry Shawnee turned and stomped off.

When the Indians had bedded down for the night, Nathan said, "I'm sorry I got you into this, Joshua. We'll never escape."

"Not right away, at least."

"We're gettin' farther away from the Ohio. And even if we could find our way back ..." A tinge of bitterness made Nathan's voice crack. "Moses Green will make everybody leave as usual early tomorrow morning."

"You're right. They won't stop all three flatboats just to hunt for us."

83

"That one Shawnee with the scar across his nose—I'm afraid he'll kill us if he gets the chance."

"Did you see the scalps hanging on his belt? He acts like we're the ones who gave him that scar."

"If I had my gun, I'd show them a thing or two."

Joshua shook his head. "Nathan, there are *seven* of them!"

"So … what do *you* think we should do?"

Joshua paused. "I think we should trust the Lord to show us what to do and the right time to do it."

"Hmmph! How will we know?"

"Well, there's a Bible verse my Grandma taught me …"

"A Bible verse? What good is that?"

"It's a promise. 'Be not afraid, for the Lord thy God is with thee, whithersoever thou goest.'"

"Maybe God's with you, but I don't think He's with *me*."

"Why wouldn't He be with you?"

"I don't know a thing about God."

"Would you *like* to know?"

Nathan thought for long while. "What better time than now?"

"God sent His Son Jesus so when we believe in Him, we can be in God's family."

"What should I believe about Jesus? I know that he was born as a baby at Christmas time."

"Yes, and he lived his whole life without any sin."

"Sin?"

"You know, the wrong things we all do."

"Like sneaking down to get the rope?"

"Right. Then Jesus died to take the punishment for *our* sin."

"Why would He do *that?*"

"There would be no other way for us to get to heaven. Think about it. He's the only perfect person."

"Yeah, but why would anyone die when they didn't have to?"

"Jesus died for us 'cause he loves us." Joshua got a lump in his throat. Explaining this to someone else made it clearer to *him.* "Oh, and Jesus didn't stay dead—God made Him alive again and now He lives in heaven."

Nathan was silent for several minutes. "Well, I do believe all that you've told me about Jesus."

"Then tell God you want Jesus to save you."

After a simple, heartfelt prayer, Nathan looked up and smiled at Joshua. "Now God's goin' to take care of both of us, right?"

"He already is! They haven't scalped us, have they? And I don't think they will, either."

"Why not?"

"They're probably going to adopt us into their tribe."

"How do you know?"

"Uncle Philip. Remember he told us the story about running the gauntlet ..."

Suddenly a loud voice came from the far side of the campfire. "Ne-pah-loh! You, sleep!"

Both boys became quiet, but neither one slept much. They were too far from the fire to feel much warmth. Their wrists and ankles throbbed from the rawhide binding. The ground was very hard. As he realized that he might never see his family again, hot tears stung Joshua's eyes. His chest had a tight knot in it where his heart usually was. *Then he remembered what Grandma Sarah had said that morning: "we learn best to trust when we're in danger." Lord, what will happen to us? Lord, help us. I'm scared. Watch over us, please, Lord.*

By the pale light of early dawn, the Shawnees loaded the boys and the gear on the horses and set off. They rode all that day with but a few stops. When they camped for the night, both boys were hungry enough to ask, by simple gestures, for more meat and dried corn. Wasegoboah nodded and brought them more food, and some water. The captives were again staked and tied before the Shawnees rolled into their own blankets. Neither boy said much as they wrestled with their own gloomy thoughts before dropping off to a restless sleep.

About noon of the following day, they came to a rushing river. The line of Indians turned and followed it north. Gradually the steep tree-clad banks softened. The trail opened into a meadow. The Shawnees stopped to give the horses a drink and let them graze briefly. To Joshua's amazement, several Shawnees waded into the river and pulled a canoe out of the shallow water near the bank. They emptied the canoe of rocks and water. Wasegoboah motioned for the boys to climb in. Two braves paddled; the rest rode off with the horses.

"We must be close to their town," Nathan whispered. "Now we'll have to run the gauntlet."

"Is that where we have to run between two lines of Indians while they hit us with sticks?"

"Yes, and if you reach their meeting house at the end of the line, then you're safe."

Both boys quivered with fear as they headed toward the village. They could see it through the trees ahead. *Wigewas* spread out on both sides of the river.

There must be hundreds of huts, thought Joshua with a sinking heart.

As the canoe drew closer, they saw a double line of Shawnee braves, squaws, and young children. The line began at the river and went up the hill for a long way to a large building. The Indians were shouting and laughing as they waved their blackberry briars or willow switches. *They're waiting for us.* Joshua closed his eyes and prayed.

Nathan groaned. "I'm scared."

"Me, too."

The sky darkened and the boys heard thunder in the distance as they climbed onto shore. Shawnees from the village met them and stripped off their shirts and shoes. *There's the map.* Joshua noticed it fall to the ground, mostly hidden by his shirt. The boys rubbed their newly freed wrists and waited, hearts pounding, staring at the scene before them. Whoops and shouts spilled from the youngsters in the line. *This is like a game day for them,* Joshua thought.

Dark gray thunderclouds rumbled closer as a Shawnee brave with a brightly decorated vest and buckskin leggings came toward them and pointed to Nathan.

"You, boy! Run!" The Indian pointed to the council house beyond the rows of Shawnees. "No stop till reach *msi-kah-mi-qui.*" He raised his stick and whacked Nathan across his back. Nathan almost fell before even taking a single step. He staggered and ran a zigzag course through the swishing switches and flying branches.

Joshua could hardly take his eyes off Nathan. "He's goin' to make it!" Then he remembered the map. He scooped it up quickly, stuffing it into his britches.

Just as Joshua looked back, Peshewa stepped forward and tripped Nathan. He sprawled on his face and immediately two braves grabbed him and dragged him back to the starting place. The second time he ran straighter, but slower. Nearly everyone had the chance to hit him. His back and arms were covered with red, oozing stripes. Finally he staggered to the open door of the council house.

C-c-crack! Boom!

Joshua jumped. *That lightnin' was really close.* Some of the squaws from the line were beginning to herd the youngest stick wavers back to their *wigewas*. Sheets of rain poured down. The same brave in the fancy vest returned and pointed at Joshua.

"You! Run! No stop till *msi-kah-mi-qui*."

Joshua took off running without waiting to be whacked and ran as if his life depended on it. The line of Indians was just as long, but it had some empty spaces now. *Thank you, Lord, for the storm.* The rain came in torrents, making it hard to see. The briars and switches cut into his back and arms. His chest was ready to burst. *The council house is so far … I can't make it. Oh, no, there's Peshewa, the one who hates us!*

He heard Nathan shouting, "You can do it, Joshua!" Peshewa heard it too, and turned to look toward Nathan for just a split-second. With a burst of speed, Joshua raced abreast of Peshewa. The young Shawnee turned back and raised his stick to hit Joshua's back, then shouted angrily when his blow barely grazed its target.

Finally, Joshua dove over the threshold of the council house, exhausted. Rain poured down outside, but both of them had reached safety. *Thank you, Lord. Now, what happens next?*

Chapter 8

Two New Shawnee Braves

Joshua and Nathan were taken to separate *wigewas*. There each one began the process of adoption into the Shawnee tribe. Methotasa, Joshua's Shawnee mother, treated him as kindly as if he were her own son. She put medicine on his cuts and gave him a blanket. She made him a hot drink, which tasted awful but helped him regain his strength. His three Shawnee brothers, Kumskaka, Sauwaseekau, and Lowaysica each nodded and spoke to him.

"You Shawnee, now!" Kumskaka said. "You stay Chillicothe!" *Chillicothe. That's the Indian town we put on my map.*

Joshua did not want to become a Shawnee but felt he should not resist. His brothers began the transformation by pulling out much of his hair, one hair at a time. The four-inch patch left on the top of his head was braided and decorated with feathers.

Joshua gradually learned his way around the village, with Kumskaka as his guide. He learned many Shawnee words.

One day, after the cuts on Joshua's back had healed, Kumskaka took him down to the riverbank. Joshua was not prepared for what happened next. Three old squaws stripped off his clothes and pulled him into the water. The squaws grabbed handfuls of the gravelly sand from the river bottom and scrubbed Joshua all over.

"Help, Kumskaka, help!" Joshua called to his Indian brother on the bank. "Make them stop!"

Kumskaka just laughed, but soon after Joshua was allowed to escape from their ceremonial cleansing. "Now all white blood washed away," Kumskaka explained.

Methotasa provided new Shawnee clothing. "From son Tecumseh," she said.

Joshua admired the deerskin leggings, shirt, and moccasins. Each had been beautifully decorated with beads and porcupine quills. He smiled and tried out the Shawnee word for thank you.

Kumskaka next brought a bowl of greasy reddish paste. Joshua looked at it suspiciously. "That stuff smells! What's it for?"

Kumskaka rubbed it on Joshua's face and arms. "You red skin like Shawnee brave."

My Indian family acts as if I've always lived here. Joshua nodded and smiled in spite of himself.

The next day, Nathan and Joshua were called to the *msi-kah-mi-qui*. "I'm a little scared," Joshua whispered. "The whole village is here." Chief Black Hoof stood and raised a hand for silence. He solemnly motioned for the two boys to step forward. Both boys' faces had been painted and they wore buckskin breeches, vests, and decorated moccasins. Their scalp locks had been braided and decorated with feathers and beads. When everyone was seated, the chief gave a long welcoming speech, which they could not understand.

"You now Nen-nemki Skilleway-thetha. Means Thunder Boy," he said, pointing at Joshua. "You," this time he pointed at Nathan, "you, Pasquawke—means Storm Clouds."

Joshua looked at his friend Nathan—*he looks just like a Shawnee. And I do too. I wonder if my own family would recognize me.* He laughed to himself. *Beka and Mary and Hannah would be afraid of me.*

Among all the friendly Shawnee faces, Joshua's eyes were drawn to a scowling face with a crooked nose. *Peshewa! He still looks as if he'd like to scalp me.* Joshua shivered.

One day several weeks later, Joshua sat in the *wigewa* trying to sort out his feelings. He watched two of his Shawnee brothers playing a game with round stones. *It has been three weeks since we were captured. Every day I've tried to figure out a way to escape. Yet it would be foolish to try.* Joshua shuddered as he recalled what happened to the white man who had attempted to escape soon after their arrival. The horrible screams as they tortured him finally ended with his death. *At first, I missed Pa and Ma and Beka and Grandma so much my insides ached. Every night when I closed my eyes, I couldn't think of anythin' else. Yet each day all the new things happenin' just pushed the sadness to the back of my mind. I still miss them all. But it's like I'm visitin' some other relatives. Kumskaka has been like a real brother to me.*

Sawaseeka burst into the wigewa. "Captives coming!"

Lowaysica quickly dropped the stick he was whittling. "Good. A gauntlet!"

Joshua squirmed uneasily. *Will they expect me to be in the line? I might know someone. Maybe someone from my own family.* His eyes met Kumskaka's.

"Thunder Boy, you watch. Stand by river." Joshua nodded and hurried to join the growing crowd near the riverbank. The stream of prisoners trudged along, carrying bundles of all sizes and shapes. Some limped. All looked frightened and very tired, as if they had been walking for days. Joshua knew they wouldn't be able to run very fast. He stared in surprise at the family just now shuffling past him. *I know them! They were on one of the other flatboats.* He continued to search the passing faces. One older man caught his eye. *Oh, no, it's Moses Green! He got captured too. Maybe I can find out about my family.* Joshua turned to watch the lines forming for the gauntlet. Kumskaka and his other two Shawnee brothers waved willow switches. Joshua wondered why he couldn't enjoy this whole thing as much as the Shawnees obviously did. *My back hurt for days after I ran the gauntlet. I don't even want to watch.* He closed his eyes and tried to think of something else. *I wonder what my family's doing now. Did they get to Limestone safely? Did Pa build us a cabin? Did he claim some farmland? Does anyone miss me?* The shouting increased and Joshua opened his eyes to watch. *They're dragging somebody back to the beginning of the line. It's Moses Green. He must have stopped, or fallen down.* As Joshua watched, Peshewa raised his stick high, then lashed the older man's bleeding back. *Peshewa shows such hatred.* Joshua closed his eyes again. *Many more prisoners are waiting their turn. Lord, help these poor people make it through the gauntlet.*

The rest of the day was a blur. It matched Joshua's mixed up thoughts. *The Shawnee Indians like to cause pain ... is it because all white people are their enemies? I'll never make a good Shawnee, no matter what Kumskaka says. But I may never escape from Chillicothe.*

A few weeks later Joshua had a chance to talk to Moses Green. The old river pilot looked skinnier than ever and limped badly. Joshua asked, "Do you recognize me, Mr. Green?"

The older man, surprised, looked at him closely. "Why, you're Joshua Stewart! Except for the blond hair, you look just like a Shawnee."

"Do you have any news of my family?"

"They're fine, I think. Limestone wasn't attacked like Ruddell's Station."

"I'm glad. I've caused them enough sorrow."

"The night you two disappeared, all the men in the party hunted till dark for you. We found a rope that Will Washburn recognized ..."

"Oh, the rope. Yes, Nathan borrowed it so we could go measure a tree."

"Measure a tree?"

"Yes, we were stupid. We should've listened to your good advice."

"We fanned out and found your trail. When we saw that the Indians were on horseback, we knew there was no chance we could catch up."

"How did Ma take that news?"

"She broke down and sobbed. Said she wished your family had stayed in Virginia."

Joshua's throat tightened and he blinked back tears.

"You know, I never did see anyone as calm as your pa and your grandma. They comforted your ma by tellin' her that the Lord was watchin' over you wherever you might be."

Joshua nodded vigorously and finally spoke. "Thanks, Mr. Green."

Joshua and Nathan had been captives in Chillicothe for two months now. Among the whites adopted into the Shawnee tribe, one man particularly aroused Joshua's curiosity. He was a leader among the Shawnees.

"Him Simon Girty. Come help Shawnees fight Shemanese," Kumskaka had explained.

"You mean, he wasn't captured first?"

"No, him trader. Live with Shawnees. Hunt with braves."

How could a white man leave civilization and enjoy living like an Indian? Oh, yes, Nathan and I enjoy spending our days roaming the woods and hunting, just like the Shawnees.

"When can I try my new bow, Kumskaka?" Joshua asked.

"Today. Get *anequoi* for roasting." Kumskaka picked up his bow and selected six arrows to put in his quiver. Joshua grabbed his own bow and followed his Shawnee brother along the trail into the woods. Kumskaka took the first shot, killing a fat gray squirrel.

"Good shot, Kumskaka."

"Now your turn."

Joshua missed more times than he hit the elusive animals. Pulling the sinew back to shoot the arrow was surprisingly difficult. They brought seven of them home that day, and Joshua helped skin and prepare them. Methotasa sprinkled some powdered seasonings on them and then wrapped them in wet cornhusks. Kumskaka placed them in the coals and carefully scraped more coals over them.

When they were done, Joshua eagerly tried a taste. "These are delicious."

"*Anequoi, oui-sah,*" Kumskaka said, rubbing his stomach.

"*Oui-sah,*" Joshua repeated, nodding and smiling and rubbing his stomach too.

As Joshua understood more Shawnee words, he learned from Kumskaka more about his Shawnee family. Kumskaka's father, Pucksinwah, was now dead, but had been a respected chief. Besides two brothers his same age, Kumskaka had two older brothers and a married sister.

"I have a sister, too," Joshua said. "But she's a little sister. Her name is Rebekah."

Kumskaka told Joshua about his two older brothers who would be coming home from a great journey, perhaps soon. "Tecumseh left as a boy, but will return as a man," Kumskaka said.

Joshua and Kumskaka went often to tend the family garden, located a short hike from the village. "Beans, corn, and pumpkins—three sisters who like to grow together," Kumskaka said. The two of them used their hoes to attack the weeds as if they were enemies of the three sisters.

Some days they went to gather berries or hunt certain wild roots for the family meal. Joshua admired his Shawnee brother's knowledge of wild plants. Joshua now recognized many medicinal plants. He could spot the many edible plants quickly, as well. *If I ever need to survive in the woods, I know how.*

Kumskaka was a patient teacher. He often stopped to point to the telltale signs that an animal had passed by. Joshua could follow an animal's trail through the woods. The freshly bent grasses, the claw marks in soft ground, the little piles of animal droppings; these told him their secrets.

One day after they had worked in the garden, Kumskaka said, "Come see hideaway place, Thunder Boy." Kumskaka led him past the last of the garden plots along a trail that led to a stream. There he showed Joshua a hollow sycamore about half as large as the one the two boys had measured on that fateful day when they were captured. They climbed inside through a hole at the base hidden by weeds.

"It's a little house," said Joshua. From then on, each time they worked in the garden, they visited their secret place. *I must tell Nathan about this sometime.*

And so the days passed quickly. As he roamed the woods with Kumskaka, it was almost possible for Joshua to put thoughts of his other family out of his mind. At night, however, as he lay on his deerskin, he thought of Ma and Pa. He wondered what Beka was doing. He thought of Grandma Sarah and the last Bible verse he had learned from her. He thought of Mary and Hannah, of Uncle Philip and Aunt Susannah and his little cousin John. It was sometimes hard to go to sleep until he reminded himself, *God has a reason for me to be in Chillicothe instead of Limestone.*

Excitement rippled across the village. It was game and feast day. The harvest of corn and beans was spread on skins or hung to dry in the late August sun. Preparations had begun days ago. There would be pony races, tests of skill and strength for all ages, and plenty of food. Kumskaka and Joshua had been practicing for the young braves' foot race for a week now. Each of them hoped to win.

They lined up with perhaps twenty-five other boys in the open area by the river. The course was about a quarter mile, Joshua guessed. Nathan, Lowaysica and Sawaseeka nodded at them from down the line. Joshua noticed that Peshewa was also one of the runners. A crowd of squaws and warriors crowded around to watch.

Suddenly Kumskaka whooped with joy and pointed to two braves in the crowd. "Look, Chiksika and Tecumseh! They return. We must run fast for my brothers."

The race was about to begin. A tall warrior raised a decorated stick, paused and hit the ground with it. At the signal, the boys rushed forward. At first, all the racers raced as one, each straining and jostling for position. The youngest boys soon fell behind; Joshua and Kumskaka were near the front, with three others ahead of them. *That's Nathan leading. Oh, no, that's Peshewa right behind him!*

Without warning, Peshewa crashed into Nathan, who tripped and went rolling. This slowed Peshewa down just enough so the other front-running brave pulled ahead and won the race. Peshewa did not disguise his anger as the winner accepted the decorated stick.

"Why does Peshewa act the way he does?" Joshua asked Kumskaka. "I know he tripped my friend Pasquawke on purpose."

"Peshewa's father die by Shemanese," Kumskaka said. "Peshewa same time got scar by nose. He hate all whites, even those now Shawnee."

Joshua shook his head. "He wants to kill me."

Kumskaka put his hand on Joshua's shoulder. "You son of Chief Pucksinwah. Peshewa not harm you. He pay with death."

Of course. Grandma always reminded me I'm a King's son, too. Joshua straightened his shoulders and smiled. "Let's go see Pasquawke, the real winner of the race."

Joshua went up to Nathan and clapped him on the back. "You ran well, Pasquawke. Kumskaka and I say you really won that race."

"Someday I'll settle the score with old Crooked Nose," Nathan said.

Joshua shook his head, frowning, but said nothing. *Be careful, Nathan. That attitude may get you killed.*

Later that day, the braves sat down to a feast—venison, coon, squirrel, green corn, and wild berries. Joshua watched his older Shawnee brothers as they laughed and talked. Chiksika and Tecumseh looked much alike. Tecumseh, though younger, was taller. Kumskaka asked them to tell about their trip. From what Joshua could understand, they had traveled hundreds of miles, both to the west and to the north. They had visited many other Indian tribes along the way.

"How you like Shawnee life, Thunder Boy?" Chiksika asked.

"Good. Kumskaka taught me to hunt and to track. He is my brother."

"Big brother Chiksika taught me much, too." Tecumseh smiled at all of his brothers. "Someday *I* be older brother, take younger brothers on great journey to learn much."

Joshua, though he couldn't explain why, really wanted to be the one chosen by this young brave. "I ... I'd like to go on a great journey someday."

"You come here from far away?" Chiksika asked.

"Yes ... I came from a place called Virginia." Joshua remembered his map, which he kept with him as a reminder of home. He pulled it from his shirt and spread it before them. "Here is a map I made which shows my village."

The Shawnee boys had never seen a map before. They puzzled over the different markings. Tecumseh pointed to the long wiggly "V" of the Ohio River and asked, "What this line, Thunder Boy?"

"That line is the Ohio River." Joshua traced the route with his finger. "I traveled from here to here on a flatboat with my family."

"Where Chillicothe?" Kumskaka wondered.

"Right here." Joshua pointed to an X north of Limestone.

Tecumseh struggled to understand all this. How river and village flat?" After a few minutes he exclaimed, "I understand! Map see as Great Spirit see, from sky."

Joshua nodded and smiled, but he was now the puzzled one. "Great Spirit?"

Tecumseh pointed to the sky and said, "Great Spirit, ruler of all things."

Joshua nodded harder. "Yes, I know the Great God who made all things. I know his Son, Jesus, too!"

"Not heard Great Spirit had son," Tecumseh said. "Where you learn this?"

"God sent a book for people to read, the Bible. It tells all about His son, Jesus."

"Someday I see this book!"

"I hope you will. It is a wonderful book," Joshua said. *I wonder if that will ever happen. The white settlers are not plannin' to give Bibles to the Indians, but bullets!*

Chapter 9

Attack of the Long-Knives

Joshua and Kumskaka were just returning from the harvest feast when they heard horses galloping up behind them. They jumped to the side of the trail and watched as the six men sped past. "Girty and Red Snake!" Kumskaka said. The riders reined their horses to a stop in front of Chief Black Hoof's *wigewa*.

Kumskaka whispered to Joshua, "Maybe big news for chief. Go, listen!"

Chief Black Hoof had fought many battles and was greatly respected among the Shawnees. The boys watched Simon Girty and Red Snake approach the chief's *wigewa* and call to him for permission to enter. The two went in, leaving the other men to hold the horses. Inside the wigewa Girty spoke urgently. "We just came from hunting twenty miles below here on the Little Miami River. We spied an army of Shemanese, long-knives—maybe a thousand. They've set up camp there and will probably attack us first thing in the morning."

Joshua and Kumskaka exchanged worried looks. There was a long silence from inside the *wigewa*. Finally, they heard the old chief speaking. "We have but one hundred warriors here today. We cannot hope to stand against such a large army. We must abandon Chillicothe." There was a sad finality in his voice.

Black Hoof called all the subchiefs. He spoke in a strong, calm voice. "We must leave here tonight. Tell everyone to pack whatever he can carry. The rest of their treasures, tools, and goods we will hide in our secret place. Then we will join forces with our brothers at Piqua Town."

Kumskaka and Joshua hurried back to their own *wigewa*. Joshua had many questions racing around in his mind.

"Where is Piqua Town?" Joshua asked Kumskaka.

"Other Shawnee town—Piqua Town—half-day's walk north. Then, fight *Shemanese*, win."

"And how soon will we leave?" Joshua noticed he'd said *we*.

"Tonight." Kumskaka said. "After treasures all hiding."

What a change came over the Shawnee village! Squaws, warriors, and children carried greased buckskin bags to the pile behind the *msi-kah-mi-qui* for hiding. Methotasa put kettles, food, furs, knives, and clothing into saddlebags for their trip. She wrapped the rest in greased skins for the boys to carry to the growing pile behind the council house.

As Joshua helped Methotasa get ready, one big question ran through his mind. *Should I try to escape tonight?* He hated to leave his Shawnee family, especially Kumskaka. Yet he yearned to see his own ma and pa and sister and grandma. *Lord, show me the answer. And show Nathan, too.*

As darkness fell, Black Hoof gave the signal for all warriors and squaws to form a line behind the council house. The line wound down a steep slope into a marshy area. Kumskaka and Joshua took places in the line. Just a few yards away, Peshewa leaned forward to glare at Joshua; he curled his lip into an ugly snarl and pulled his finger rapidly across his throat.

He plans to kill me ... I must escape tonight, or else! In silence, Joshua concentrated on passing one bundle after another to Kumskaka. The last one in line, Chief Black Hoof himself, leaned over and dropped them into a deep, dark pool. Splunk! Splunk! Splunk! One after another, the village's treasures disappeared.

Joshua knew he must take action soon. *Maybe Pa or Uncle Philip is in that army that's coming. Maybe they are coming to rescue us.*

As Joshua tried to think how he and Nathan could safely escape, an idea came to his mind. *We could start out on the march to Piqua Town and disappear into the woods. We'd need a place to meet.* Joshua gave this a few minutes of thought, and then almost shouted out loud as the answer came to him. *The hollow tree! It's near the garden area. Nathan knows how to get there ... but how can I tell him without makin' everyone suspicious?*

Again, it took several minutes of sorting through ideas to come up with a good plan. *I'll cut off the blank end of my map and write Nathan a note.*

Joshua set to work right away. He cut the fabric with his knife. Charcoal from the fire ring made a handy pencil.

LEAVE MARCH LINE MEET IN HOLLOW TREE TONIGHT.

Joshua rolled up the message and put it inside his shirt. He hoped to see Nathan among those scurrying around the village.

Going to Nathan's *wigewa* might arouse suspicion. *Time's gettin'* *short. Lord, bring Nathan across my path,* Joshua prayed. He looked up from his prayer to see Nathan walking toward him.

"Ho, Pasquawke," Joshua said, "Secrets." He quickly slipped Nathan the scrap of cloth and continued walking. Nathan looked after Joshua with surprise. Then he looked around to make sure no one was watching, unrolled the map and read the instructions. He nodded, smiled, and tucked the cloth inside his shirt.

It was long after midnight when all preparations for abandoning the village were complete. Joshua's growing tension gave him a stomachache. Escaping would be a slap in the face to those he had come to care for, especially his brother Kumskaka. He wished he could at least say good-bye, yet he dared not hint about his plans.

Methotasa had prepared a bedroll for each of her sons. Joshua and Kumskaka picked up theirs and set out to join those already leaving Chillicothe. Tecumseh called out as they passed, "Thunder Boy, you take journey now. Learn much."

Joshua stopped and turned to reply, then changed his mind. *I am learnin' that leavin' my Shawnee family is tearin'* *out a piece of my heart.*

The line stretched ahead as far as Joshua could see, which wasn't very far. The moon was merely a sliver. The path wound northward through the trees. No one used a torch. Those who talked spoke in low tones.

"I am sorry about this, Kumskaka," Joshua said as they crossed to the far edge of the village.

"Army coming, we leaving, Thunder Boy," Kumskaka replied.

Kumskaka walked just ahead of him in the line. *Does he suspect something? How can I slip away with Kumskaka so close?*

Joshua turned for a last glimpse of the Indian town. He stared. The sky was glowing red! "Look, Kumskaka, Chillicothe is burning!" Joshua felt a stab of sadness for his adopted family. *Now they can't go back.*

"Yes, Shawnees burn village each time *Shemanese* come," Kumskaka replied.

They walked on in silence. *I need to hang back from Kumskaka and the others who know me*, Joshua thought. He sat down and took off his moccasin, as if to shake out a pebble. He waved to Kumskaka to keep walking.

Kumskaka looked at Joshua for a long moment then shook his head. "I stay with you."

Joshua got up again and picked up his bedroll. They continued to march silently along the dark trail. *What should I do, Lord? I guess I'll just wait for a chance to slip into the woods.*

The line began to stretch out as the path became narrower. After half an hour, the path took a sharp turn through thick underbrush. Joshua stepped behind a large tree. He quickly crept far back from the trail and headed toward the gardens. He crawled into a hollow tree at the bottom of a ravine and waited. Off in the distance he heard his name. "Thunder Boy … Thunder Boy!"

It's Kumskaka. The young Shawnee came closer, still calling out Joshua's name. It took every effort of Joshua's will *not* to answer back. He thought of the times when they had been out in the woods together. They would often call to each other after going off in different directions to hunt. Now they must be forever separated.

Kumskaka's voice faded away, but Joshua knew he must wait. Half an hour later, Kumskaka came back past Joshua's hiding place, headed toward Piqua Town. Joshua hoped his brother would rejoin the rest of the Shawnees. After another half hour, Joshua left his hiding place and crept through the underbrush toward the trail leading to the gardens. *I wonder if Nathan got away.*

As he walked along the familiar path, Joshua relaxed a little bit. The quarter moon looked like a smile, so he smiled back. Ahead, the garden plots stretched for several miles. Joshua looked around hopefully for his friend. *Everythin' looks strange and shadowy at night. I don't see Nathan.* He picked a handful of beans to nibble on, and then walked in the direction of the hollow tree.

Suddenly, an owl hooted from behind him. *Or was it an owl?* As he turned to look, Joshua caught a movement out of the corner of his eye. *It must be Nathan!* He almost called Nathan's name, but something made him uneasy. He quickly ducked behind a large corn patch.

Is there someone in the shadow? He strained his eyes; at first, he saw nothing. Then one of the shadows moved. *It is someone, but who? Not Kumskaka. It could be Nathan, but … no.*

A Shawnee brave stepped into the dim light of the moon, moving noiselessly toward the spot where Joshua crouched. Fear gripped his heart as Joshua recognized who it was. *Peshewa! He must have followed Kumskaka. He waited until I came out of hidin' and followed me.* Joshua crawled along toward the safety of the hollow tree. *If I can keep out of sight, maybe I can make it to the tree.*

He glanced behind him. *Peshewa is getting closer!* Joshua stood up and began running, still keeping as low as possible. Ahead loomed the dark shadows of the woods. *If I can make it to the path ... I'll cut over to the hollow tree.* Joshua left the last patch of corn and raced across the open area to the safety of the trees.

"AAIIEEE!!" Peshewa's bloodcurdling scream ripped open the silence.

Joshua ran for his life, his heart pounding from fear. He turned to see how close his opponent had come. Peshewa was one step behind. *Lord, help!* Suddenly Joshua tripped on a tree root. He hit the ground with a thud, sprawling along the path. He struggled to catch his breath and stand again, but Peshewa was poised to leap on his back. Even in the dim light Joshua could see the sneer of triumph on his face. The Shawnee raised his tomahawk and took a flying leap toward his enemy. Joshua rolled out of the way, but Peshewa's tomahawk still sliced a long gash in his upper arm. Joshua scrambled to his feet, running. *He will catch me soon ... what do I do next?*

"*Matchele ne tha-tha!*" Peshewa shouted.

You are my enemy, too, Joshua thought, panting and straining to run even faster.

The next moment, Peshewa grabbed Joshua from behind and pushed him facedown to the ground. Joshua felt the sharp pressure of Peshewa's knee in his back. He tried to twist free.

"*Matchele ne tha-tha!*" Peshewa shouted again as he pulled Joshua's head backward by his scalp lock. He raised his tomahawk high in the air.

He's going to scalp me! Joshua struggled even harder, trying to free himself from the grip of the Shawnee brave. At any moment, he expected a searing pain in his forehead.

Suddenly, another figure hurtled toward them, grabbing Peshewa's upraised arm. The Shawnee turned to grapple with this unexpected opponent, letting go of Joshua's scalp lock. Joshua twisted to see his rescuer. *Kumskaka! Of course ... the owl call warning!* Kumskaka kicked Peshewa, trying to get him off Joshua's back.

Joshua escaped from Peshewa's grip and struggled to his feet.

"Run, Thunder B—!" Kumskaka shouted. Peshewa grabbed the young brave around his neck, choking him and cutting short his warning.

I can't leave my brother ... Peshewa will kill him! Joshua gripped his knife, hesitating just a moment. The fear he had felt at first was gone. He took a deep breath, determined to rescue his Shawnee brother.

Peshewa's arm tightened around Kumskaka's neck and he raised his tomahawk. Joshua leaped toward them and plunged his knife into Peshewa's side. Screeching horribly, Peshewa released Kumskaka and lunged toward his attacker.

Joshua jumped back from Peshewa's swishing tomahawk just in time. Kumskaka barreled into Peshewa from the back, catching him off balance. He staggered to the ground. "Run, Kumskaka!" Joshua shouted.

Both boys ran this time, in opposite directions. Joshua raced toward the hollow tree. He glanced back and saw Peshewa holding a bloody hand against the deep gash in his side. The angry Shawnee's attention was turned toward the fleeing Kumskaka. *Perhaps Kumskaka will double back and join me at our tree. He saved my life!*

Joshua soon reached the safety of the hollow tree. He bent down, shoved the weeds aside, and wriggled up through the opening. *Safe.* He gripped his knife and listened for any sound of Peshewa, but heard only his own racing heartbeat. Joshua felt limp and barely able to move. He had hoped to find Nathan waiting for him. Joshua reached up to touch the painful gash on his upper arm and felt the warm blood still oozing out. *"Ouch!" It is only because of Kumskaka that I'm still alive. I hope I see him again. Thank you, Lord, for sendin' him at just the right time. Help me to know what to do tomorrow.*

Homeward
Bound

Joshua thrashed around as he tried to get out of a vivid dream. He was running through the woods. Peshewa was chasing him. Running, running. The Shawnee waved his tomahawk and shouted *Matchele ne tha-tha!*

"Unnh," he groaned, now fully awake. His shoulder throbbed, a sharp reminder that the nightmare had been real. *What next? Maybe Nathan is still with the Shawnees. And did Kumskaka get safely to Piqua Town?*

Joshua peeked out of the hiding place. The sky showed the first bright pink streaks of dawn. *No warning calls from the jays or squirrels ... guess it's safe to come out. Oww, my arm hurts.*

His deerskin shirt had a long slash. Dark red blood had dried on it, gluing the shirt to his skin. Joshua headed to the stream and carefully washed the cut, then removed his shirt.

Hmm, not as bad as it could be. He twisted around to look at the wound. He took a long drink, realizing suddenly how hungry he was.

Joshua started back along the path toward the gardens. *I think I can find the spot where I tossed my bedroll ... no sign of Peshewa, that's good.* Suddenly Joshua stopped short and stared. *This is where I stabbed Peshewa. The blood on those leaves is probably his blood.* The struggle of the previous night came back vividly to his mind. *Kumskaka saved my life. I wish I could thank him.*

Further on, Joshua retrieved his bedroll from the weeds of his first hiding place. Some jerky and some more garden beans filled the empty spot in his stomach. *Now to figure out what to do …*

Joshua hiked to the main trail and looked northward. *The Shawnees are probably all the way to Piqua Town by now … so maybe Nathan is hidin' out somewhere between here and there.* Joshua headed north again, along the same path he'd traveled with the line of marchers the night before. He looked carefully for anything Nathan may have left as a signal … *maybe the map end.* Beaten-down grasses showed that a large number of people and horses had passed this way just hours before. *But was Nathan among them?*

Suddenly, he heard a shout from somewhere behind him. "You, boy … halt!"

Joshua whirled around, but saw no one. "Nathan?"

Two frontiersmen with rifles pointed toward him stepped out of the woods. "Who goes there?" the larger of the two demanded.

Joshua dropped his bedroll and raised his hands. "Don't shoot! It's … Joshua Stewart."

The men lowered their rifles. One was as big as a bear and had a red beard. He strode toward Joshua with his hand stretched out. "We been lookin' fer you, Joshua!"

"Why? Who are you?"

"We're scouts with Colonel George Rogers Clark's army. My name's Simon Kenton. This here's Jacob Miller."

"I've heard your name before, Mr. Kenton. My uncle, Philip Bradley, said you're the best woodsman in Kentucky. But why were you lookin' for me?"

"We're headin' to Piqua Town to scout it out, and I just had a hunch you were one of the two boys captured last spring."

"Iffen you hadn't said somethin', Simon, I was fixin' to shoot him fer a Shawnee!" Jacob interrupted with a laugh.

"You're purty brave, now, ain't ya? This boy don't even have a rifle," Simon chided his fellow scout. He turned to Joshua. "Where's Nathan Washburn, the other boy captured at the same time?"

"We both tried to escape last night, but he wasn't at our meetin' place."

"Looks like you met up with *somebody*, and not too friendly!" Jacob put in.

Joshua glanced at his arm and nodded. "I think Nathan may be hidin' somewhere along this trail, or maybe he's with the Shawnees in Piqua."

"And so you were going to rescue him?" Simon asked. When Joshua nodded, the scout demanded, "Do you s'pose that you can just turn around and leave town once you've found him?"

"Haw, haw!" Jacob chortled.

"That arm of yours needs attention." Simon turned to Jacob, "I'm takin' him back to camp. You meet up with the other two scouts and bring your report as soon as possible."

"Yessir, Captain Kenton."

"But what about Nathan?" Joshua asked.

"Your friend may be back in Chillicothe and already safe and sound. C'mon with me back to the horses." Joshua climbed up behind the scout. They waved good-bye to Jacob and galloped toward Chillicothe. They rode in silence at first, and then Simon asked, "Are you ready to see your family again?"

"Yes, of course … but it was still hard to leave my Shawnee family."

"Your Uncle Philip is worried about you."

"Is he in the army?"

"Yes. So is Nathan's pa."

"And my pa?"

"I convinced your pa to stay back in Limestone to help protect the settlement. Your parents are worried about you."

Joshua's eyes filled with tears. *It must have been hard on them all the time I was gone … not even knowin' for sure whether I was still alive.* Joshua suddenly wanted to see his Ma and Pa, Beka, and Grandma Sarah again so much that it hurt.

Simon continued, "The army is busy destroying the Shawnee gardens and cornfields around Chillicothe."

Joshua thought of the times he'd helped in the garden. *What will Kumskaka and the others eat this winter?* "Will they attack Piqua Town next?"

"That's the plan. They'll probably attack tomorrow or the next day. Colonel Clark knows that this army hankers to fight some Shawnees. They'd be mighty upset if they didn't get to."

Joshua kept silent for as long as he could, and then asked, "But why can't the army just go back home and leave the Shawnees alone?"

It was Simon's turn to be silent. Then he turned and looked at Joshua. "You know, it warn't too long ago that I was livin' in that same Shawnee village of Chillicothe. Near lost my life there. I know the Shawnees first hand. They'll fight the settlers till the last Shawnee is dead. So it's either us or them."

Joshua didn't answer, but he had a sinking feeling in the pit of his stomach.

When they reached Chillicothe, Joshua was shocked to see the charred remains of what had been his home until a few hours ago. Acrid-smelling smoke hung in the air. He closed his eyes to the ugly sight and tried to picture the new log cabin that would be waiting for him in Limestone. *I must leave the Shawnee part of me right here.*

Soon after they rode into camp, Captain Kenton headed for the medical tent. Uncle Philip burst out the front of it before Joshua had even dismounted.

"Joshua!" Uncle Philip pulled him down and started to give him a bear hug.

"Ow! Watch out for my arm."

Uncle Philip shook his head sadly, "Another casualty." He turned to the scout.

"Thanks for findin' him, Captain Kenton. I was worried that I'd have to go back to his parents empty-handed." He rubbed Joshua's topknot with a laugh. "But I don't know how they'll take to having a Shawnee son."

Joshua laughed too and turned to his rescuer. "Yes, thank you, sir, for bringing me to my uncle. But I'm still worried about Nathan."

Uncle Philip tugged on Joshua's good arm. "C'mon inside the tent. I've got a surprise for you."

"Nathan! You did escape," Joshua hurried over to his friend. "What happened to your shoulder?"

"I got shot."

Uncle Philip laughed, "Yep, Nathan escaped from the Shawnees without a scratch, but one of our Kentucky sharpshooters winged him."

Nathan smiled a little. "Guess he thought I was a Shawnee. It's funny … I always wanted to shoot Indians. Now I know what it's like to get shot."

Nathan's father stood to his feet from the stool beside his son. "We need to get these boys home to their mothers."

"Maybe Colonel Clark can spare one of us to ride back with them." Uncle Philip suggested.

"I'm not leavin' till I get to shoot some Shawnees!" Nathan's pa said. "After what they did to my son."

"First, let's get that arm of yours fixed up, Joshua. I'd be honored to escort these two *former* Shawnees back to Limestone, then," Uncle Philip said with a laugh.

The three of them, on two horses, were heading south along the beautiful Little Miami River within the hour. The boys recognized much of the scenery from their trip along the same route four months ago. Both of them realized they had changed in many ways in that time.

"Do you still think that Shawnees are savages, Nathan?" Joshua asked.

"No. My Shawnee family was really kind to me. My Shawnee brother taught me lots about animals and about how to use plants as medicine."

"I learned how to track an animal or even a person through the woods," Joshua said.

"I learned to track, too. I won't need a hunting dog when I go after a bear this fall."

Joshua turned to his uncle and asked, "Tell me about Ma and Pa and Beka and Grandma. How are they doing?"

"Well, your ma's been movin' a bit slower these past few months. You're getting a baby brother or sister very soon!"

Joshua's mouth dropped open. "That's right! Ma did say something about our family growing."

Nathan teased, "Poor Joshua! You might end up with two sisters, like me."

"Limestone was gettin' together to raise the Stewart cabin a few days after I left with Colonel Clark's army."

"I forgot to ask Pa whether we had a cabin yet," Nathan said.

"Your pa managed to get your cabin raised before he left to fight Shawnees with us."

"I hope it's like the one we saw on our first day on the Ohio."

"Your family had been living in the flatboat cabin for more'n a month," Uncle Philip laughed, "so anythin' would be an improvement."

The trio camped beside the Little Miami River that night. After dinner, they sat around the campfire talking.

"I wanted to escape from Chillicothe, but part of me wanted to stay," Joshua said.

"I felt the same way. I don't know why," Nathan admitted.

"My Indian mother treated me just like I was really her son."

"Yes, mine, too."

"And the night we escaped, Kumskaka saved my life." Joshua told how Peshewa had chased him through the woods and nearly succeeded in scalping him. "But I was able to help my Indian brother get away, too, by stabbin' Peshewa in the side."

"Good! I always wanted to get him back for trippin' me in the race."

"I think someday maybe I'll go back," Joshua said.

"Why, Joshua?" Uncle Philip asked.

"To thank my Indian brother for saving my life, to see my Shawnee family, to see Chillicothe …" He stopped, gazing off in the distance.

Uncle Philip poked the fire and added some new wood. "Chillicothe is gone now."

"Yes, but they'll come back," Joshua declared.

"I agree. They'll at least come for all that stuff they hid in the swamp," Nathan said. "But I never want to see the place again!"

Uncle Philip nodded. "I can understand that. You two are finally goin' to Limestone."

"Yes, we've never even seen it." Nathan leaned forward with excitement.

"As we get closer to home, I'm getting more and more excited about seein' my family," Joshua added.

Nathan nodded in agreement. "Joshua, God really did take care of us, like you said."

They sat back and watched the sky change from rose, to crimson, and then fade to shades of blue and purple.

Thank you, Lord, for safety for Nathan and me. Keep Kumskaka and his family … my Shawnee family … safe when the army attacks Piqua Town. Joshua gazed at the sunset sky. *Help me have peace in my heart about my Shawnee family. Amen.*

Next morning, Uncle Philip and his two charges broke camp and headed south again. "We'll probably reach the Ohio River by evenin'," Uncle Philip said.

"Then it's one more day to Limestone?" Nathan asked.

"Yep."

"It's takin' us a long time to get there," Joshua said.

Uncle Philip laughed. "I'm sure your families are going to be surprised when I ride up and deliver an Indian to each cabin."

The sun rose higher and hotter. Joshua's arm still throbbed from his wound and Nathan could barely ride. Both boys had aching muscles from the half-day's ride of the day before, yet neither one wanted to stop early.

The sun was low in the sky when they stopped for the night. There below them was the wide Ohio River. It sparkled as if inviting them to come for a closer look.

"You boys go down to the river and get us some water. I'll take the horses over to that grassy area and stake 'em." He pointed to a natural meadow a quarter mile away.

The boys had to push their way through saplings and blackberry bushes to get down to the river. As they picked and ate the ripe berries, Nathan whispered, "Look at that, will you."

Not far ahead of them, two good-sized bear cubs were feasting on blackberries. They stuffed berries into their mouths, and then scampered to the next bush. One bear batted playfully at the other, who turned and swiped his brother's nose to defend himself. The boys watched for several minutes, enjoying the show.

Suddenly they heard a grunt behind them. Horrified, they saw the mother bear just a stone's throw away. She stood on her hind legs, sniffing the air. She looked huge.

"Look at those claws," Joshua whispered as the boys ducked low.

"What'll we do?" Nathan asked.

"These trees aren't big enough to climb …"

"Bears can climb trees anyway."

Joshua said, "Let's split up. She can't chase us both."

"The one that gets away can go get your uncle's gun."

"Crawl. Maybe she won't see us." Joshua began creeping to the left, trying to keep the bear in sight. *She's movin'.* The bear suddenly charged toward the place the boys had just left. *Wow! She covered that distance in two bounds! I'm glad I'm not there anymore.*

Now the bear stood on her hind legs and sniffed. She put sound and smell together and charged in Joshua's direction. *Lord, help me!* Joshua realized he could not outrun the angry mother bear. *There's a big stick.* He grabbed it and turned to face the animal. "*Go away! Leave me alone!*" he shouted, waving the stick wildly. The bear stopped, surprised. Joshua's heart pounded and his legs felt like rubber, but he stood his ground. He waved his weapon and shouted again. The bear snarled and took a swipe at the stick.

Next Joshua heard Nathan shouting from the top of the hill. The bear heard him, too, and turned to run in Nathan's direction. Joshua took this chance to escape, clawing his way to the top of the bank. With both boys out of sight, the bear returned to her cubs and began feasting on blackberries as if nothing had happened.

"That was a close call! Thanks for saving my life," Joshua said.

"We never did get any water," Nathan laughed.

"I think I'll just stay thirsty. My knees are still all wobbly."

When Uncle Philip heard their story, he praised them for their quick thinking. "Now you boys will have your own bear story to tell your sisters," he laughed.

After a quick supper, they decided to ride further before camping for the night. "We've had enough excitement for one day," Uncle Philip said.

It was suppertime when the tired trio rode into Limestone. Earlier in the day, they had crossed the Ohio River upstream from the settlement. The horses eagerly plunged into the current; Uncle Philip said it was because they could tell they were getting close to home.

"Look there, boys. The settlement is a mile from this spot. We've come here to fish a few times." Joshua and Nathan, sharing the same horse, shared a feeling of excitement, too.

"My ma is going to jump for joy when she sees me," Nathan predicted.

Smoke drifted from the chimneys of the cabins they passed. Dogs began to howl. Uncle Philip waved to the settlers who poked their heads out to see why their dogs were barking. "We've rescued our lost boys!" he called out to everyone.

"Your cabin's dead ahead, Nathan. See it there beyond those evergreens?"

As they neared the crude log structure, they heard a loud shriek. "That's Mary!" Nathan said.

"You two wait here; I'll go up first and tell your ma she's not being attacked by Shawnees!" Uncle Philip dismounted.

He needn't have worried, for the door burst open and everyone ran out, shouting with joy.

The tearful family reunion that followed made Joshua in a hurry to get to his own cabin. Nathan's ma kept repeating, "You're home safe … I can't believe it!" She laughed as tears ran down her cheeks. She turned to Uncle Philip and said, "Thank you, thank you for bringing them home! When will my William be coming back?"

"They have to finish off the Shawnees before they come back, but I imagine that won't take too long," he replied.

Joshua felt a stab of pain as he thought of Kumskaka and the others. *I wonder if they're safe.*

Nathan's sisters crowded up to their brother and began asking questions. Mary gave Joshua a strange look, as if she didn't recognize him anymore.

After what seemed like enough time to skin a dozen squirrels, Uncle Philip and Joshua headed to the Stewart cabin. As they rode along the streambed below the cabin, they saw Beka with a bucket. "Hullo, Rebekah!" Uncle Philip shouted.

She stared, then waved, then dropped the bucket and ran back up the hill to the cabin, shouting, "Here comes Uncle Philip with an Indian!"

Everyone ran to the cabin door and crowded for a look—Pa in his stocking feet, Aunt Susannah wiping her hands on her apron, Little John squealing "Papa's home!" Ma and Grandma Sarah … all wanted to make sure Rebekah wasn't imagining things in the twilight. Zeke began barking loudly, not sure if this stranger was friend or foe.

Now it was Ma's turn to shout. "That's no Indian; that's Joshua! Praise the Lord!"

"Here comes riding an answer to prayer," Grandma Sarah said.

"Make that two answers to prayer," Susannah said.

As soon as the two of them were off the horse, they were overwhelmed with hugs, kisses, and questions. Everyone laughed, cried, or talked to Joshua.

Uncle Philip held up his hand. "Whoa! You'd better feed us first, so we'll have the strength to tell you all our stories." He turned to wink at Joshua as they all went inside.

"You're not the only ones with something exciting to tell," Ma declared. "Joshua, come and see your new baby brother." She pulled the corner of the blanket back to show a tiny face with two bright eyes and light brown hair. "His name is Caleb Philip." Uncle Philip grinned proudly.

"And you have another sister now, too, Joshua." Beka brought a second baby over for them to see. "Isn't she beautiful? I helped name her. Her name is Esther Rose."

"T-two babies?" Joshua looked from one to the other.

"Twins! That's more exciting than our stories. I guess we'll just have to keep quiet, eh, Joshua?" Uncle Philip asked.

The rest of the evening was spent hearing Joshua's tales of Shawnee life with Kumskaka, and Philip's yarns about soldiering with Colonel George Rogers Clark. Joshua told the story of how Nathan saved him from the bear. Pa told about the cabin raising. Ma and Beka talked about their garden.

Finally, it was time to blow out the candles and head to bed. Grandma Sarah summed up how everyone felt. "Our cup of blessing is just running over!"

Chapter 11

Whithersoever Thou Goest

"What was it like to live with Indians, Joshua?" Beka called out to her brother as they scrambled down the hill behind their cabin to explore "their" stream.

Sunlight filtered down through the trees, and the stream splashed quietly over the rocks. Zeke trailed along behind, sticking his nose under rocks and jumping back in surprise if anything wiggled.

Joshua walked to the water's edge and pointed. "Look at these tracks in the mud. Kumskaka taught me all about the tracks of wild animals."

Beka squatted down beside her brother and looked at the paw prints. "So what kind of tracks are these?"

"A big raccoon came down here just a few hours ago, maybe to wash his food."

"Really?" Beka picked up a pretty stone to put in her pocket.

"I learned to track almost as well as Kumskaka. Sometimes we'd spend the whole day in the woods."

"Did you *feel* like an Indian?"

"In some ways, yes. But the Shawnees' way of thinking is very different from ours."

"What do you mean?"

"A Shawnee will treat another Shawnee very well, but Shawnees enjoy causing pain to an enemy." Joshua bent down and picked up three flat stones and skimmed them across the water. "Remember Moses Green? He was one of the prisoners that were brought to Chillicothe from that settlement the Indians burned. There was another family from the second flatboat, too. Those poor prisoners had marched for days and looked half dead. But they all had to run the gauntlet."

"Is that when the Indians stand in a line and hit you with sticks? Uncle Philip told us about that."

"Yes. The Shawnees treat it like a celebration or a sport. They give the prisoner a chance to run, so they think it's fair."

"You and Nathan ran through a gauntlet?"

"Yes. Everyone that the Shawnees adopt must prove their bravery that way."

Beka shuddered. "I'm glad you're safely back home again."

"Me, too." Joshua picked up a stick and began drawing in the mud. He drew the squiggly V of the Ohio River, and then put an X for Limestone. Beka leaned over to watch. Joshua then scratched another X, for Chillicothe. "I might go back someday, though."

"No!" Beka cried. "Don't you *ever* go away again!"

"I won't go away any time soon, don't worry."

"But why would you ever want to go back? It would be dangerous."

"Remember you told me what Grandma Sarah said? The Lord had sent me to Chillicothe for a reason."

"Yes, but ..."

"Well, I think I know the reason." Joshua drew a connecting line between the two Xs.

He looked at his sister. "The Shawnees need to know about Jesus."

Beka was quiet for a long time, and then asked. "Would they listen?"

"Tecumseh, one of my Shawnee brothers, told me they believe their Great Spirit rules all things. I told him the One who made all things has a Son, Jesus."

"So they know about God, but not about Jesus?"

"No. They don't have the Bible, so their Great Spirit is not the same God that we worship." Joshua drew one more line, making a cross. "Someday, somehow, I want to tell them about Jesus."

"Do you think Ma and Pa would let you go?"

"I don't know." Joshua threw his stick into the water, where it landed with a splash. "You're the first one to hear about my idea."

Beka smiled uncertainly. "I'm not sure I like it." Then, as if to change the subject, she ran ahead, calling, "Follow me. You can talk to Ma and Pa later."

"I want to tell Grandma Sarah, too. She will understand the best, I think."

The two of them spent the rest of the afternoon exploring the stream behind their cabin. They were surprised when they heard the clang, clang, clang of the dinner bell.

After dinner, Pa gathered them for family worship. Beka and Joshua sat on the floor. The twins were asleep in their double cradle nearby. Grandma had the Bible open in her lap since it was her turn to read the Scripture.

Pa leaned back in his chair. "Tonight, let's begin by counting our blessings."

Ma laughed, "We won't ever get to the Bible reading, we've got so many."

"Amen to that," Grandma added. "I'll go first. I'm thankful to the Lord for bringing Joshua home safely."

"Me, too," Beka said.

"Beka, you have to think of a different one," Joshua said.

"That's easy. I'm thankful for Esther Rose."

"And I'm glad that I finally have a brother. Thank you, Lord, for Caleb."

Ma smiled. "I'm thankful for all of those blessings and our own cabin."

Pa nodded. "Bless the Lord, O my soul, and forget not all his benefits. My blessin', on top of all the others, is finally havin' land I can call my own."

Ma began singing Psalm 128, and they all joined in.

> Everyone that fears the Lord,
> Fears the Lord, fears the Lord,
> Everyone that fears the Lord
> Has blessings all the day.
>
> He'll eat the labor of his hands
> Of his hands, of his hands,
> He'll eat the labor of his hands, and
> Happy he shall be.
>
> Wife and children all around,
> All around, all around. With
> Wife and children all around,
> Happy he shall be.

"Here's the Bible reading for tonight," Grandma said. "Romans 10:13-15, 'For whosoever shall call upon the name of the Lord shall be saved. How shall they hear without a preacher? As it is written, how beautiful are the feet of them that preach the gospel of peace.'"

Pa asked, "How shall we apply this to our own lives?"

"I called upon Jesus to ask Him to save me," Beka said.

"I think we should pray for a preacher for our own settlement, so all the people can hear and believe," Pa said.

"As Caleb and Esther grow up, we must teach them about the Lord so they can know Him," Ma said.

Joshua sat up straighter and glanced at Beka. "I think the Lord wants me to go tell the Shawnees about Jesus."

Nobody said a word for a long minute. Ma had tears ready to spill down her cheeks. When Esther began to fuss, Ma jumped up right away to get her.

Grandma was the first to find her voice. "The Lord's had his hand on you for a long time, Joshua. I'm just thankful He's allowed me to live long enough to see this day."

Ma finally was able to speak, though her voice quavered. "Joshua, I think it's wonderful … that you have been called … to be a missionary to the … Shawnees."

Pa struggled with his thoughts. "The time when you could take the gospel to the Shawnees is some years away, of course. Son, I'm proud of you."

Ma came up behind Joshua and put her hand on his shoulder. "The Lord still has other big lessons to teach all of us. Right now, son, *you're* the teacher."

Epilogue

You may wonder what happened to some of the people you met in this story. Joshua, Nathan and their families faced many challenges as early settlers in Limestone. Perhaps Joshua became a circuit-riding preacher who frequently carried the gospel to Shawnee villages. Nathan married and lived on the frontier, showing a kind heart toward those Indians he met. Their younger siblings, Beka, Esther, Caleb, Mary, and Hannah helped settle new areas of the frontier and had adventures of their own.

Simon Kenton and Tecumseh were two men who actually lived on the frontier. Their paths came together several times before they died. Simon Kenton ran away from home as a teenager when he thought he had killed a man in a fistfight. For many years he went by the name of Simon Butler. When he learned that the man had survived, Simon took his own name again. Simon Kenton continued to help settlers by protecting them against Indian attacks. He settled later in Kenton's Station, not far from Limestone. In 1795, Kenton attended the signing of the Greenville Treaty, which officially ended the Indian Wars. Twelve different tribes, represented by many chiefs, signed the treaty.

One who did not attend nor sign the treaty was the young Shawnee chief, Tecumseh. He felt that these agreements were worthless. When Tecumseh learned the Indians were again being pushed off their lands, a cold determination was born in his heart. With the help of his younger brother, Lowaw-Luway-Sica, (shortened to Lowaysica in our story), Tecumseh gathered all the tribes together to fight the last great Indian war against the whites. During the war's final battle, Tecumseh died, as his father Pucksinwah had died before him, bravely leading Shawnee warriors.

In 1808, Simon Kenton attended another meeting where many men found peace. This one was a Methodist Episcopal camp meeting. Settlers came from miles away to Voss's campground near Springfield, Ohio. Preachers stood on stumps or hillsides and called on men, women, and children to confess their sins and take the Lord Jesus as Savior. As Simon listened, he remembered the sins of his full life and feared that he was not prepared to die. He confessed his fears to a preacher as they walked in the woods, warning the preacher to tell no one. Simon knelt with him in the woods to pray the sinners' prayer. When the Lord saved him, Simon jumped up from his knees and ran to shout the news to his wife, relatives, and friends. Now he wanted everyone to know. "If I had all the world here, I would tell of the mercy and goodness of God!" Simon declared.

LaVergne, TN USA
19 July 2010
189982LV00002B/3/P